Mahabharata Stories

Mahabharata Stories

Deepa Agarwal

Illustrations by
Megha Punater

HarperCollins*Children's Books*

First published in India in 2019 by HarperCollins Children's Books
An imprint of HarperCollins *Publishers*
A-75, Sector 57, Noida, Uttar Pradesh 201301, India
www.harpercollins.co.in

2 4 6 8 10 9 7 5 3 1

P-ISBN: 978-93-5357-328-7

Typeset in 13/19 Century at
Manipal Digital Systems, Manipal

Printed and bound at
Thomson Press (India) Ltd

This book is produced from independently certified FSC® paper to ensure
responsible forest management.

For my beloved grandchildren Adya, Kartik,
Aanya, Anika and Ahan

Contents

How the Mahabharata was Written

Veda Vyasa sat under the shade of a great banyan tree. It was a hot, still day. The air was so oppressive that even the birds who nestled in the trees were silent.

The learned sage was silent too. He was an impressive sight, with his flowing white beard and the thick knot of hair crowning his head. The strings of enormous rudraksha beads that hung around his neck and were wound around his forearms and his saffron robes marked him as a man of religion.

His disciples were ranged around him – young men, some mere boys, with shaved heads on which the tufts of their shikhas or topknots were prominent. Their eyes were fixed on their guru. Some looked puzzled, others anxious for Vyasa to begin the day's lessons. But the sage's mind seemed elsewhere. His large, hypnotic eyes gazed unseeingly into the distance and his wide brow was furrowed with lines of worry.

The disciples glanced at each other questioningly. But the sage continued to be preoccupied. All of a sudden, he nodded slowly and a faint smile flitted across his face. He seemed to have found a solution to his problem. It was a knotty one indeed. It had weighed on his mind night and day, disturbing his sleep at night and his concentration during the day.

Vyasa, known as Krishna Dwaipayana because of his dark skin and the fact that he had been born on a dweep or island, was the son of Maharishi Parashar and the fisher girl Satyavati. He was also called Veda Vyasa because he had divided the Vedas and organized the Vedic hymns. A man blessed with great knowledge, Vyasa had been granted a vision by Brahma the Creator himself. This vision led Vyasa to compose a vast epic, a great heroic poem.

When the poem was complete, who should turn up but the travelling sage Narada?

'Narayana, Narayana!' he greeted Vyasa, strumming the tambura that he always carried.

'Narayana, Narayana, Narada Muni!' Vyasa replied enthusiastically. 'You've arrived at a very auspicious time. Please lend an ear to my new creation.' And without waiting for an answer, Vyasa began to recite his great work in his sonorous voice, all 18,000 shlokas (verses) of it. It took a few days, but time was under the control of the great sages. The rigorous penances they had undergone had given them special powers. Hence, days felt like hours to them.

'Narayana, Narayana! What an extraordinary work!' exclaimed the adviser of the gods, when Vyasa was done. 'It is magnificent, Vyasa. Unique! But you must write it down. That way, it can reach all mankind. There is so much in it that will be of benefit to them.'

'Why shouldn't I just teach it to my disciples?' Vyasa replied. 'They will recite it at gatherings in different places and people will hear it. Thus, it will spread throughout the world.'

'Teach your disciples, definitely,' Narada agreed. 'But writing will give it not only permanence but also accuracy. No matter how good a person's memory might be, it can play tricks. Some important parts might be forgotten or distorted in the retelling.'

'It's an enormous work, Narada,' Vyasa objected. 'Who will be able to take it down completely? Is there anyone who will be equal to the task?'

Narada clicked the khartal he always carried impatiently. He rose, ready to be off again. 'That is a problem you will have to solve yourself, respected Vyasa,' he said, whizzing off on his magical self-propelling slippers.

This was indeed the problem that had been preoccupying Vyasa. Who was capable of writing down his immense work? And then, a thought flashed across his mind. Who could advise him better than

Lord Brahma? After all, Lord Brahma was the one who had granted him the inspiration to compose this epic.

The thought had barely taken shape when the benign form of Brahma appeared before him. His prayer had been answered! Vyasa hurriedly got to his feet. He folded his hands and bowed low before the Creator. His disciples followed suit immediately.

Brahma raised his hand in blessing. Then he sat down. 'Come sit beside me, boys,' he said kindly. 'What is bothering you so much, Vyasa? You look extremely worried.'

'You inspired me to write a great poem, Lord,' Vyasa began.

'So I did,' Brahma nodded. 'Is it complete now? What all have you included in it?'

'It contains everything possible,' Vyasa replied. 'It tells of the past, present and future. It describes all the mysteries of life like fear and disease, death and decay.'

Brahma nodded again, smiling. 'That's excellent!' he said. 'Have you put in anything about your great work, the Vedas?'

'Yes, Lord,' Vyasa replied. 'I have explained in brief the philosophy of the Vedas and the Upanishads. Also, I have brought in the dimensions of heavenly bodies like the stars and planets.'

'What about the rules of conduct?' Brahma wrinkled his brow. 'I hope you haven't forgotten that. You know how important dharma is for the world to run smoothly.'

'No, I haven't,' Vyasa said. 'I have set down all the rules of conduct not only for the four castes but also for ascetics. I have also described the four Yugas or epochs. And the science and the healing of sickness have been included too.' Vyasa stopped to think for a moment. 'I have also given a definition of charity and how it should be practised.'

Lord Brahma's interrogation did not stop there. 'And what about the subject of reincarnation?' he asked.

'That is discussed in my work too,' was Vyasa's prompt reply.

'What else have you put into this vast work?' was Brahma's next query.

'I have described mountains and rivers, forests and lakes and all the places of pilgrimage. Even the art of war is explained in detail. Different nations of the world, their languages, the qualities of their people find mention too. Not to forget the spirit of humanity that pervades all.' Vyasa paused to draw breath. Then his brow darkened with anxiety. 'I have not left anything important out, Lord ... but I am faced with a serious problem now. Who in this universe possesses the ability to pen down this enormous composition?'

'I am extremely pleased with what you have accomplished, Vyasa. It sounds like the greatest work in all creation,' Brahma beamed, immensely pleased. 'I don't think any other poem composed can possibly be its equal. You want someone to put it into writing, you say? Who could be better than Ganesha? He is the most intent listener. Why don't you ask him?'

Vyasa's face lit up as if touched by the first rays of the sun. Brahma's suggestion was excellent. Ganesha would be the ideal person.

'Many thanks, Lord, for your blessed guidance!' Vyasa folded his hands and bowed low in gratitude. 'You have given me sound advice, as always. I shall ask Ganesha.'

Vyasa immediately began to make preparations to welcome Lord Ganesha. He set out a platter piled with the elephant-headed god's favourite sweet, modak. He heaped another platter with fruit. Then he began to pray fervently to Ganesha, the god who had the power to remove all obstacles.

And soon his prayers were answered. Ganesha appeared, riding his mouse, Mushaka.

Vyasa bent low in greeting. 'Greetings to you too, learned sage,' Ganesha replied. 'Why have you summoned me today? What is it that you wish from me?'

'You have come a long way, Lord,' Vyasa replied. 'Please refresh yourself first. Try these modaks. I know you love them.'

Ganesha smiled. 'You are a man after my heart. You think of everything.'

After Ganesha had demolished half the modaks and was rubbing his belly contentedly, Vyasa made his request in the politest of voices. 'My Lord, there is something I wish to share with you. I have composed a vast poem, which I have titled "Jaya". All humanity will gain much benefit from the knowledge of this work – for generations to come.'

'It sounds like a great work. But how can I help you?' Ganesha asked.

'The poem is complete in my mind. But to preserve it in its original form, I need someone to write it down as I recite it. Lord Brahma said you would be the right person,' Vyasa said, looking at Ganesha hopefully.

Ganesha nodded slowly. 'Hmm ...' he said. Then a mischievous smile hovered at the corner of his mouth. 'It will be a pleasure to take down such an extraordinary poem. Only, you will have to agree to a certain condition.'

A condition! Vyasa was somewhat perplexed. Why a condition? Suppose he was unable to fulfill it? But then ... who could be a better scribe than Ganesha himself? There was no harm in finding out what he wanted.

'As you wish, Lord,' Vyasa replied diplomatically. 'Please tell me what it is.'

'It is a small thing for a person of your intellectual calibre,' Ganesha smiled again. 'But if you do not comply with it, I won't write.' He paused to take in Vyasa's expression, then continued. 'While you are reciting, you must not pause at all. My pen must not halt while I write, not for a single minute. If you are sure you can manage it, I agree to take on the role of your scribe.'

Vyasa chewed his lip for a moment, thinking. The poem was more or less complete in his mind. But it would be impossible to rattle off such an enormous work without pausing to think even for one minute. He glanced at Ganesha and caught the gleam of challenge in his eyes.

He had to meet the condition, whatever it took! But was there some way he could reduce the pressure on himself?

And then, it came to him. Yes, there was a way. He should impose a counter condition. Something that would slow down the god's writing speed and grant him respite.

'I agree, Lord Ganesha,' he bowed respectfully. 'But if you permit, I have a small condition too. You must understand the meaning of what I dictate before you write it down. Each and every verse of the epic should be clear in your mind.' He paused to stroke his beard thoughtfully, then continued. 'Because what is the point of penning down words whose meaning you have not grasped?'

Ganesha could not suppress a smile. Vyasa had been wily indeed. But he replied, 'I am willing to accept your condition. Now tell me when you are ready to begin.'

Vyasa did not wish to waste any time. 'If it suits you, in just a few minutes,' he said. He beckoned to his disciples. 'Go, my sons, hurry and bring the writing materials. As quickly as you can.'

The disciples ran off. Within minutes, they were back with scrolls of birch bark, quills and ink.

Then Ganesha sat down comfortably on a low stool. He intoned the sacred word 'Om' sonorously, so it resounded all through the hermitage. Vyasa drew a deep breath and began to chant the epic, at breathless speed.

He dictated stories of gods and demons, great sages and powerful kings. Of men, wise and noble, foolish and evil, women possessing virtue and intelligence, with scheming minds and sharp tongues. He described heroic deeds while he narrated the accounts of deadly battles, as well as acts of cowardice and treachery. He also worked in complex philosophies, the art of living wisely and the rules of righteous conduct into these stories.

Ganesha's pen flew like magic over the scroll, taking it all down without a single pause, barely allowing Vyasa time to breathe or even think. Feeling the pressure, Vyasa then took refuge in a trick. Whenever he felt he could not keep up with Ganesha, he would compose difficult pieces of verse. Terse passages packed with subtle shades of meaning. Complex words, in which the slightest change of stress on one syllable could alter the interpretation altogether. Even the all-knowing Ganesha had to stop and think, and in the meantime, Vyasa got the respite he needed. While Ganesha halted to deliberate, Vyasa quickly composed a few more verses.

The elephant-headed god, however, was eager to complete this task as soon as possible. He did not want even a minute's delay. In a matter of time, it became like a race between the two – whether Vyasa could recite faster or Ganesha write quicker.

And then it happened. As Ganesha was writing at breakneck speed, his pen broke. But the god was not one to be deterred by such an obstacle. Looking around for the first pointed object available, he found it was his own tusk. Without hesitating for a second, he grasped his left tusk and snapped off the tip. He then dipped it into ink and continued to write.

So, this is how Ganesha lost his tusk. He sacrificed it in his quest to write the Mahabharata, or 'Jaya' as the original work was known, as fast as possible.

And at such super speed, the longest epic in the world—one hundred stanzas in verse—was written. Dictated by one of the most learned sages, Veda Vyasa, and transcribed by the god of auspicious beginnings, Lord Ganesha himself.

The Art of the Mritasanjivani

It was a pleasant spring day. The sun shone bright but not too warm and a gentle breeze stirred the air.

Devyani, the daughter of the sage Sukracharya, happened to glance out of the window. She noticed a young man approaching their hermitage.

Sukracharya was the guru of the Asuras or demons. He lived in the capital city ruled by Vrishaparva, the king of the asuras.

Who could this man be, Devyani wondered idly? He was rather good-looking and his polished manner showed that he was well-bred. Was he a new pupil, eager to seek knowledge under her father's guidance? Curious, she strolled out and began to busy herself gathering herbs close by.

The youth walked up to her father, who sat thumbing his beads under the majestic banyan tree in front of their house. He folded his hands and made a low bow. 'Greetings, most respected guru,' he said in a musical voice.

Sukracharya stretched out a hand in blessing. 'Please introduce yourself, young man,' he said kindly. 'And do let me know what I can do for you.'

'Respected sir, I am Kacha, the grandson of Angiras and the son of Brihaspati,' the young man replied. 'I have heard much about the extent and depth of your knowledge. It struck me that I could benefit a great deal from your teaching. Please accept me as your student, kind sir.'

Devyani noticed her father's start of surprise and guessed the reason. The moment the youth introduced himself as Brihaspati's son, her brow had wrinkled automatically. Brihaspati was the guru of the devas or gods, who were the enemies of the Asuras. Why did his son want to come under Sukracharya's tutelage?

She knew, however, that whatever misgivings her father might have, he would not refuse Kacha. The teacher's code of ethics did not permit him to turn away a prospective pupil.

Stroking his long beard thoughtfully, Sukracharya replied, 'I am deeply honoured that your father chose me as your teacher. He himself has immense knowledge of the scriptures. When learning runs in your blood, I cannot help wondering if there is anything new that I can teach you. All the same, I will be very pleased to accept you in my hermitage.'

A broad smile lit up Kacha's face and his eyes gleamed with gratitude. He bowed to the ground again and again. 'Words cannot express my gratitude, noble sire,' he said, his voice trembling with joy. 'I will do my best to prove myself worthy of a teacher like you.'

'You will be part of my household,' Sukracharya said. He noticed that Devyani was nearby and beckoned to her. 'Kacha, this is my daughter Devyani.' The sage's eyes lit up as he said this. He was very fond of his daughter. 'My child, please bring some refreshments for our guest.'

Kacha folded his hands to greet her and Devyani smiled and bowed to him before she hurried to do her father's bidding.

Little did Sukracharya or Devyani know that Kacha had come to the ashram with a specific purpose. He had come to learn the extraordinary art of Mritasanjivani. Sukracharya was the only person in all three worlds who possessed this precious knowledge. He knew how to bring a dead person back to life.

At that time, the gods and the demons were engaged in a struggle for supremacy of the universe. In this fight, Sukracharya's knowledge of the Mritasanjivani gave the Asuras a great advantage. No matter how many Asuras the Devas killed, Sukracharya was able to bring them all back to life. This meant that the gods could never outnumber them in battle. For this reason, they were desperate to acquire this knowledge at any cost. After consulting Brihaspati, they came up with the plan to send Kacha to Sukracharya as a disciple to try to get hold of this important mantra.

Several months went by and Kacha turned out to be the perfect student. He performed all his duties well and served his guru devotedly. He was also a quick learner and regular with his studies. Besides this, he demonstrated great proficiency in the art of music and dance and in his spare time, he would entertain Devyani. His performances charmed her so much that soon she found herself falling in love with him. However, as was the custom, Kacha had taken the vow of brahmacharya, which meant that he had to maintain a distance from women. So, his behaviour towards her was exemplary. He always treated her like a sister or friend.

The other Asuras had not been as welcoming as Guru Sukracharya. They had been suspicious of Kacha right from the beginning, convinced that he had come to steal the Mritasanjivani mantra. When they questioned Sukracharya about taking him as a disciple, the sage had reminded them that he was compelled to follow the code of conduct of a teacher and thus could not refuse Kacha's request. Hearing this, the Asuras decided to take matters into their own hands and do away with Brihaspati's son.

One day, following his usual routine, Kacha went to the forest to graze Sukracharya's cows. The Asuras followed him stealthily. When he was all alone, they pounced on him, tore his body to pieces and fed it to the dogs.

In the meantime, back at the ashram, Devyani was waiting impatiently for Kacha to return. The day felt long and dull to her without him around. When dusk began to fall, the hour for the cattle to return home arrived, and Devyani's eager eyes stayed fixed on the path that led to the forest. But the minutes passed by, the shadows lengthened, and still there was no sign of Kacha.

When will he arrive, Devyani thought anxiously. The sun has set and he is still lingering in the forest. Doesn't he realize how much I miss him while he's away?

She began to pace outside the hermitage restlessly. Her father had begun to perform his evening fire sacrifice. Usually Kacha would be back by that time to assist him. He was always so punctual. What could have delayed him, Devyani wondered.

As she gazed at the path that led from the forest, she heard a cow lowing and her heart leapt with joy. Then the whole herd came into view, churning up dust with their hooves. She darted forward eagerly, but all the cattle passed and there was no sign of Kacha.

A chill fear clutched Devyani's heart. What could have happened to him? She wanted to run and tell her father, but she was loath to disturb him at his prayers. Somehow, she controlled herself and herded the cows into their shed and poured water into their drinking trough.

She had just finished when she noticed that Sukracharya had completed his worship. Devyani rushed to him immediately. 'Pitashri!' she cried, 'the cattle have returned alone, Kacha has not come back with them. I-I'm afraid … Could he have suffered some mishap? There are wild animals in the forest.' Her eyes filled with tears.

Sukracharya's brow knotted with concern. 'That's extremely strange,' he said. 'He always accompanies them.'

'Oh father, I'm sure some calamity has befallen him! Why else is he missing?' Devyani began to weep. 'You have to do something to find out! He is one of your most dedicated disciples.'

Sukracharya stroked her head lovingly. 'Don't worry, my dear. Everything will be all right.'

He retreated into the shadows and intoned the Mritasanjivani mantra in a low voice.

After a while, he called out to Devyani, who sat in a crumpled heap near the path, her head thrust into her knees. 'Look who's come, my dear!'

Devyani looked up and cried out in joy, 'Kacha!'

It was Kacha trudging down the path. He looked troubled and confused but remembered to bow low to his teacher.

'Thank heavens, you're back,' Devyani heaved a trembling sigh. Kacha somehow produced a smile. 'What took you so long?' Devyani went on. 'You cannot imagine how anxious I – we were.'

Kacha looked fearfully at Sukracharya who had his eyes fixed on him. 'I-I am sorry to have upset you,' he stammered. 'But ... a terrible danger befell me. As I was tending the cows, some Asuras attacked me. They tore me apart and I could feel my spirit leaving my body.' He drew a deep breath and looked at his guru. 'Then, to my surprise I found myself standing all alone in the forest, alive and whole. It had turned dark but the Asuras were no longer around, and the cows had vanished too. I was terrified that they might have taken the cows away too, so I rushed back as fast as I could to find out.'

'Oh ...' Devyani almost collapsed on the ground.

'Do not worry, you can see I am breathing and alive,' Kacha smiled wanly.

Sukracharya looked grim, however. 'They would not dare to touch my cattle, even if they had the temerity to attack you. Wash your hands and feet and come inside. It is time for the evening meal.'

It was a big relief to Devyani that her father had restored Kacha to life. But the danger from the Asuras hung over his head. Sukracharya began to send another of his disciples to take the cows to the forest, saying that Kacha should concentrate on his studies.

Devyani was grateful that she could continue to enjoy Kacha's company. Because of his vow of brahmacharya she did not disclose her feelings to him. Deep inside, however, she felt that he must have guessed.

Then one day, when Devyani mentioned how she loved a particular wildflower, Kacha decided to go and pluck some from the forest for her.

In his enthusiasm, he forgot that the threat to his life had not vanished. The Asuras who had killed him earlier were extremely frustrated when Sukracharya revived him. They decided to lie in wait for another opportunity. The moment they saw him entering the forest again, they pounced on him and hacked him to death. This time they pounded his body into a paste and mixed it with the sea water. They were sure, after they had dissolved it in the vast ocean, Sukracharya would not be able bring him back to life again.

When Kacha did not return from the forest, Devyani was overcome with an even greater anxiety. She went to her father and said, 'I fear the Asuras have found him again. It's all my fault. I should have stopped him from going to the forest.'

Sukracharya could not bear to see his beloved daughter in tears. 'Wipe your eyes, Devyani,' he said. 'I will bring him back.' Once again he used his mantra and within a short time, Kacha came walking down the path.

'Young man, you need to be careful,' Sukracharya said gravely. 'Do not take any more unnecessary risks.'

Kacha folded his hands and bowed deeply. 'I am extremely grateful to you, my guru,' he said. 'It was extremely foolish on my part. I promise not to venture beyond the ashram anymore.'

But one day, a playful calf ran out of its shed and Kacha chased after it. The pursuit led him out of the ashram and the Asuras, who had been keeping watch, caught hold of him at once. They dragged him away and killed him brutally. This time, they burned his body. Then they took his ashes and mixed them in wine. Then they cunningly presented the wine to Sukracharya, saying, 'Respected sage, the king has sent this special wine for you with his compliments. He hopes you will like it.'

Sukracharya drank the wine without suspecting anything amiss. However, when Devyani saw that Kacha was nowhere to be seen, she hurried to her father.

'I'm afraid they've done away with Kacha again,' she sobbed. 'Why can't they leave the poor boy alone? He never harmed anyone.'

Sukracharya sighed heavily. He said in a troubled voice, 'My dear Devyani, I've restored him to life twice. Our fellow Asuras are determined to finish him off and I suspect they have a good reason for it.' He paused and gazed at Devyani, whose eyes were overflowing again. 'You are a sensible girl,' he said gently. 'You know every being born on this earth has to die some time. Wipe your tears. Forget Kacha. You are young and life has so much to offer you.'

Devyani could not be consoled, however. She was too deeply in love with Kacha. 'I'm surprised how calmly you accept his death, father,' she said. 'Don't you have any feelings for someone who served you so faithfully? I cannot forget him. Without Kacha, my life is meaningless. I would rather die than live without him.'

To prove her statement, Devyani began a rigorous fast. She refused all food and water and after a couple of days she became faint and listless. Sukracharya could not bear to see his daughter in this condition.

He went and sat at her bedside and said, 'Devyani, you know how precious you are to me. Please accept a glass of water for my sake. Give up this fast. I am furious with the Asuras for laying hands on my disciple, a man under my protection. And as you say, he did them no harm. Get up, child. I will restore Kacha to life.'

Devyani's sunken eyes sparkled with joy. She gulped down the water her father offered her and agreed to eat some fruit.

Sukracharya chanted the Mritasanjivani mantra once again. But to his astonishment, Kacha did not appear. How could he? He was scattered through Sukracharya's body! He did reply, however, when the sage called out his name.

When Sukracharya heard Kacha's voice resounding from within his body, he was stunned. 'Where are you, Kacha?' he asked.

'I-I'm inside you, respected guru,' Kacha replied in a faint voice.

'How did you enter my body?' Sukracharya asked. 'The Asuras have done something unforgiveable this time. I feel like leaving them and joining the Devas. Tell me, Kacha, how did this happen?'

With great difficulty, Kacha explained how the Asuras had killed him and burned him and mixed his ashes in wine. Sukracharya's eyes blazed with fury when he heard how he had been tricked.

'The wicked ones said that the king had sent a special kind of wine for me and I believed them, like a fool. Indeed, wine is the source of all evil,' he proclaimed, cursing the drink. 'No brahmin should consume it. Virtue and wisdom will flee the man who consumes it. From this day, I forswear wine.'

The problem, however, had not been solved. Deeply perplexed, the sage addressed his daughter, 'My dear Devyani, I just don't know what to do. If Kacha has to live he has to tear his way out of my body. That means certain death for me. There is no other way. For Kacha to live, I will have to give up my life.'

'No, father!' Devyani cried. 'I cannot allow that! I will not be able to bear it if you die. Oh, who could be more unfortunate than me? You are the two people most dear to me and one has to die for the other to live. That means death for me too since I cannot live without either of you.'

Sukracharya went silent, not knowing what to say to that. It was the thorniest dilemma he had faced in his life. For a long moment, he sat there, utterly cast down as Devyani wept silently.

Suddenly, he looked up. 'My child,' he began hesitantly. Devyani looked up, a flutter of hope lifting her heavy heart. Had her wise father discovered a solution?

'I have thought of a way,' he said with a reassuring smile. 'There is a way that will ensure life to both of us.'

'What is it?' Devyani started up eagerly.

'I have understood it all,' Sukracharya said. 'Kacha, I realize now that you came here with a hidden purpose—to gain knowledge of the Mritasanjivani mantra—and fate has played into your hands. For Devyani's sake, both of us need to live. If you are to emerge from my body whole, you will have to tear it apart. But I will share the art of Mritasanjivani with you. After you come out you must chant it and bring me back to life again.'

'O father, you have a solution for everything!' Devyani cried out, overjoyed.

Sukracharya then taught the secret art of the Mritasanjivani to Kacha. Soon, Kacha tore his way out of his guru's body alive and whole. Sukracharya, however, fell to the ground all mangled and torn. Immediately, Kacha made use of his newly acquired knowledge and the sage came back to life.

Kacha bowed low to his guru. His face shone with gratitude. 'A teacher is like a father,' he said. 'But I consider you my mother as well, since I was reborn from your body.'

Devyani was happy once more. Kacha continued his education with Sukracharya for some years and the Asuras left him alone now.

Then his term of study came to an end and he prepared to return to his family.

Kacha's vow of brahmacharya was also over, since he was entering the next stage of his life and he could now get married. Devyani felt this was the time to declare her love for him. When Kacha came to say farewell, she said, 'Dear Kacha, you might have guessed my secret by now. Ever since you came here to live as my father's pupil, I have fallen deeply in love with you. I did not disclose it, however, because of your vow of brahmacharya. Now I hope you will agree to marry me. I am sure your respected father Brihaspati will be pleased to welcome me as a daughter-in-law.'

However, Kacha looked embarrassed. 'Dear Devyani, you are one of the most kind and beautiful girls I have ever met. I have much affection for you and respect you greatly too,' he said gently. 'But I have been reborn from your father's body. For this reason, I consider you my sister. Please forgive me, but I cannot marry you.'

Devyani was stunned. She had not expected this response from Kacha. She tried to persuade him to change his mind. 'You are Brihaspati's son, not my father's,' she insisted. 'Remember, I was the one who convinced my father to bring you back to life because I loved you so much and wanted to marry you. It was because of my efforts that you gained knowledge of the Mritasanjivani mantra. How can you reject me now?'

Kacha was not moved by her words. 'I am extremely sorry,' he said, shaking his head. 'Devyani, you are a lovely girl and any man would be happy to marry you. But the day I was reborn I said that I considered Guru Sukracharya both my father and mother. It would be very wrong for me to take you as a wife. I must leave now. Please take good care of my noble guru.'

Devyani gazed at him, astounded. She had waited for this man for many years and had saved his life not once but three times. And now he was walking away from her in this unfeeling manner! A terrible anger took hold of her.

'Kacha, I curse you for treating me so shabbily. You will never be able to make use of the knowledge you gained through my efforts. The art of Mritasanjivani will never work for you!' she screamed in a fury.

The words fell on Kacha like a hammer blow. 'I do not deserve this,' he said in a low voice. 'My reasons for refusing to marry you are genuine. Well, if I cannot use the Mritasanjivani, I can teach it to others. For your unfair words, I curse you too. You will never be able to marry a man from your own community. No brahmin will take you as a wife.'

Kacha walked away, leaving Devyani brokenhearted. What a peculiar quirk of fate it was that denied Kacha to her, she couldn't help thinking! By saving his life, she had lost his love. Sukracharya tried to console his daughter as best as he could, but it took Devyani a long time to get over Kacha.

The Birth of Devavrata

King Shantanu was hot on the chase, pursuing a deer. The fleetfooted animal raced out of the forest towards the banks of the Ganga river. Shantanu, the ruler of Hastinapur, spurred his horse to follow it. His eyes were fixed on his prey, but suddenly something distracted him.

It was the sight of a woman, taking a leisurely stroll by the river. Shantanu reined in his horse and halted at once. The woman aroused his curiosity.

There was something mesmerizing about her. Who could she be? Her long, open hair rippled down her back and she walked with a smooth grace, as if she was floating on the sand. Could she be a heavenly Apsara come to earth? Her beauty was so enchanting that she did not appear human.

The king dismounted. 'Greetings, lovely lady,' he said, folding his hands. 'I am King Shantanu, the ruler of Hastinapur, descendant of the great King Bharata. I have never seen you here before. Please, will you tell me who you might be?'

A fleeting smile touched the woman's lips as she returned his greeting. 'I am known as Ganga, noble king,' she replied simply.

'Ganga,' the king repeated. 'Ganga, I have never come across a woman as beautiful as you. You are here all alone, do you have a family? Are you married?'

Ganga shook her head enigmatically. 'No, king, I am all alone,' she said gently.

Shantanu was puzzled. It was quite unusual for a young and good-looking woman to be roaming the riverside all by herself. But from the moment he set eyes on her, he had felt irresistibly drawn to this mysterious woman. He took a deep breath, quite conscious that what he was about to say was rather rash and impetuous and might astonish, or even offend Ganga.

In a low, hesitant voice he began, 'You say you have no family … so I'm asking you directly … will you marry me, O Ganga? Please do not refuse. I offer you not only my undying love, but also everything I own. My kingdom, my riches, even my life.' He was about to kneel before her when she stretched out a hand to stop him.

For a few moments Ganga remained silent, with her large, lustrous eyes fixed on Shantanu, then she said, 'I will marry you, O king, but only if you agree to my conditions.'

'All your conditions are acceptable to me,' said the infatuated king without a moment's hesitation.

'Please listen carefully first before agreeing,' Ganga replied in a calm voice. 'You must never ask me who my family is and where I come from. Neither you nor anyone from your household will question my actions. You must never raise your voice in anger at me or do anything to make me unhappy. If you are unable to fulfill any of these conditions, I will leave you and go away.'

'I don't care who your family is or where you come from,' Shantanu said impatiently. 'And why would I want to question your actions? It would also be absolutely unthinkable for me to speak angrily to someone I love so much,' the king continued. 'I swear by my honour as a king of the Bharata dynasty that I will abide by all these conditions.'

'I agree to be your wife then,' Ganga smiled.

The king was beside himself with joy. He took Ganga back to his palace and married her with much pomp and show. When she turned out to be the perfect wife, he congratulated himself on his excellent choice. Ganga was indeed most loving and kind. She conducted herself with grace and modesty and performed all the duties required of her as a queen faultlessly. She was so considerate and good natured that everyone in the king's household could not stop singing her praises.

As time passed, each day seemed better than the last and the king felt he had been specially blessed by the gods in finding a wife like her.

When Ganga informed him that she was expecting a child, Shantanu's happiness knew no bounds. He awaited the birth of the child eagerly. Would it be a son who would succeed him on the throne of Hastinapur, or a daughter as beautiful as Ganga? In the meantime, he pampered his queen, saw to it that she received the most nutritious and tasty food and showered her with expensive clothes and jewels.

It was a golden time for King Shantanu, each day full of joyous expectation. The months passed and at last the queen's labour pains began. The king paced up and down outside her chambers waiting for the news. How long would it take for the baby to be born? How he yearned to set eyes on it! He tried to divert himself by imagining their life with the child, watching it grow and all the activities he would plan for their young one. It felt as if life could not be more perfect.

The thin cry of a newborn baby startled him. Shantanu was thrilled to the core of his being! His first-born child, what a loud voice it had!

A maid hurried out of the queen's room, beaming all over. She bowed low. 'Congratulations, your majesty! You have been blessed with a son.'

The king's heart overflowed with happiness. Immediately, he removed a valuable pearl necklace from his throat and handed it to the maid. Overcome with gratitude, she bowed low over and over again. 'May the young prince be blessed with a long life,' she cried. 'May the gods shower all their blessings on him.'

Shantanu, however, was already rushing into the queen's chambers. But when he entered the room, he stopped short, surprised. All the maids stood around with frightened looks on their faces. They dropped their eyes when they met Shantanu's questioning gaze.

'What's wrong?' he frowned. Then he noticed that the bed was empty. Ganga was missing.

'Where's the queen? And my son?' He looked around hopefully to see if someone else was holding the baby. But there was no sign of the newborn either.

The king's brow knotted even more deeply. 'Where are they?' he roared.

The attendants shivered. They cowered together, unable to speak. 'I asked you a question,' said the king. 'Will you answer or shall I have you whipped?'

The younger maids began to wail when they heard this. Then the oldest and most trusted maid held up a hand to stop them. 'Your majesty,' she said softly, with folded hands, 'soon after the birth, just as we sent you the news, the queen got up and hurried out of the room with the baby in her arms.'

'What? Are you insane? Is this a conspiracy? I have never heard of such a thing.' Shanṭanu's face was red with rage.

'It is true, your majesty, as true as I stand here,' the maid replied gravely.

'Your majesty,' one of the other maids said in a trembling voice. 'You can see her from here …' She pointed to the window.

Shantanu rushed to the window and looked out. He could see Ganga clearly, holding a wrapped-up bundle in her arms. The baby! A chill descended on Shantanu. What was she doing? A hundred terrifying thoughts entered his mind. Which kind of woman would pick up her newborn child and go away just like that? Was she unhappy in the palace? She had never given any such indication. She was always smiling, ever loving and kind. Their life together had been perfect so far, and the baby seemed to be the ultimate blessing that would complete their happiness. Something must have frightened Ganga. He had to find out.

Without pausing for a moment, Shantanu dashed out of the door. He ignored the cries of his guards and hurried after Ganga. He had to find an explanation for this extraordinary behaviour. As he hurried down the path that the queen was taking, he realized she was headed for the river. Why was she going there? Amid the confusing jumble of thoughts that crowded his head, he remembered that he had first met her there. What was the connection?

Shantanu broke into a run, worried that he might lose sight of her. He caught up with his wife just as she reached the river. He froze with shock at what he saw there.

Ganga was placing the small bundle in the river. Shantanu's eyes dilated with horror as he watched the swift current carry his baby son away. He wanted to reach out and jump into the river to save his child, but he was too stunned to move.

'Why?' his mouth framed the words, but just in time, he remembered his promise. The memory of the conditions Ganga had imposed on him when she agreed to marry him, rose to confront him. She had said he was never to question any of her actions. How bitterly he regretted it now! But if he had not consented, she would not have married him. A terrible pain lanced King Shantanu's heart. How blind he had been, what a besotted fool! A sob burst from his throat.

He controlled himself somehow. He needed to see what Ganga would do next. To his utter amazement, she turned to meet his horrified gaze calmly. This was not the expression of a woman who had just done away with her newborn child. She looked utterly serene and unruffled.

Who was she? What was she? Had he been entrapped by a demoness disguised as a beautiful woman? It had happened to many.

Shantanu's head reeled. He sank onto a rock on the bank of the river and buried his face in his hands. His sorrow was an unbearable weight, too heavy for him to bear. His perfect life had proved to be an illusion. What would he do now? Should he banish Ganga from his kingdom? But ... the awful truth burst upon him – he could not, because he still loved her more than his life.

The cool touch of a soft hand interrupted the agonized thread of his thoughts. With an effort he looked up, still dazed with grief. Ganga met his eyes with a gentle smile, that same mysterious smile he could never fathom.

'Come, my king,' she said softly. Shantanu tottered to his feet. He followed her like an unthinking child, back to the city.

His attendants received him with cries of relief. Their eyes examined Ganga fearfully. But she still had that calm, inscrutable look on her face. No one dared to raise the question that tormented each one of them.

Shantanu spent the following days in an anguished stupor, feeling that his life had fallen apart. What troubled him most was the fact that he could not bring himself to hate Ganga. And she went on as if nothing had happened! As if it were the most natural thing for a mother to drown her newborn. If possible, she was even kinder and more attentive than she had been before. She comforted him in his most agonized moments, rubbed soothing balms into his throbbing head, sang to him in her enchanting voice, and ordered the most delectable dishes for him.

It took a long time, however, for Shantanu to recover from the shock. At night, he was tormented by terrible dreams. He would awake and gaze at her face, apprehensive that she might have transformed into a terrible fiend. No normal woman could have performed such a dreadful act and shown no signs of sorrow or remorse.

Time passed and King Shantanu's trauma abated somewhat. Ganga's loving behaviour and his own passion for her brought the smile back to his face. And then, he discovered that she was pregnant again.

Despite the terrible experience, Shantanu could not control his joy. Surely that was an aberration, he convinced himself. She will not do it again, not for the second time. She is such a loving person, my Ganga!

Once again, he spent the months of her pregnancy in a haze of joy. A niggling fear would sometimes rear up to trouble him, but he suppressed it firmly.

At last, the day came when another son was born and another wave of excitement swept the palace. However, once again Ganga picked up her newborn and hurried to the river. An anguished Shantanu followed her, hoping against hope. Once again, he stretched out an imploring arm to stop her. But his vow sealed his mouth. He had to watch the river carry away his second child and did not dare object, no matter how piercing the pain.

Once again, Ganga returned with that enigmatic smile and comforted the grieving Shantanu. Silently, he bore the loss of his second son, wondering why the gods were testing him in this manner. Once again, he wondered why he was still so much in love with Ganga, despite these cruel acts of hers. The mystery of her origin plagued him, but recalling his vow, he silenced all the questions that rose to his lips.

The extraordinary thing was that despite his horror at the fact that she could calmly drown her newborn babies, he could not bear the thought of parting from Ganga. He would not be able to live without her, he felt.

The years went by and Shantanu helplessly watched Ganga place five more of their babies in the river. The agony was unbearable but he did not dare to do anything to save them.

And then the eighth child was born. Shantanu felt now that he could not stand it any longer. He had reached the end of his tether. What use was her love? If she really cared for him, she would not kill their children so remorselessly. At the very least, she would explain her unnatural actions. Had she no pity for his suffering? Was she utterly heartless? He had to put an end to this and save his eighth child.

Once again Shantanu followed Ganga to the river as she carried away the newborn baby. The moment she bent to place the infant in the water, he cried out, 'Stop! I cannot see you do this to our children. How can you do this terrible thing? Can't you spare me at least one child?'

Ganga halted and looked up at him. Slowly she rose and smiled at him sadly. The king glared back, red-eyed and trembling with helpless rage.

'My dear husband, you know I love you deeply,' Ganga said, meeting his gaze steadily. 'But you have forgotten your promise. I have no choice now but to leave you.' She sighed as though the prospect made her unhappy. 'Your desire to save this child is stronger than your love for me. I owe you an explanation, however. Beloved king, I am the goddess Ganga.'

'The goddess Ganga!' The king was even more stunned now. 'You-you married me!' He was overwhelmed with a terrible feeling of regret. Why couldn't he have had more patience? The goddess Ganga herself had been his wife and now she would leave him! He should have understood that there must be a strong reason behind such unnatural actions. But what could he have done? He had to save one of their children at least. 'I have been truly blessed to have you as a wife, dear goddess. But now that you're leaving, you must answer this question – why did you drown our babies?' he asked.

'These eight children were the eight Vasus,' she said. 'The divine beings who were attendant deities of Indra. They were cursed to be born as mortals by the sage Vashishtha because they stole his cow, Nandini.'

'But how did all this happen?' the king asked.

'The Vasus were roaming about near Vashishtha's ashram,' Ganga began. 'One of their wives caught sight of Nandini, born of the wish-fulfilling cow, Kamadhenu. The desire to possess it took hold of her. Nandini's milk had a magical quality – it would grant immortality to whosoever drank it. The Vasus and their wives were immortal, but the wife wanted it for a mortal friend. The sage was not present at the time, so seizing the opportunity, the Vasus stole the cow. When Vashishtha returned, he was outraged to find his beloved Nandini missing. He soon discovered who the thieves were. Furious, he cursed the eight Vasus to be born as mortals.'

'But why were you chosen to be their mother?' Shantanu asked.

'The Vasus apologized for their action and pleaded for mercy,' Ganga replied. 'The sage relented and proclaimed that seven of them could be freed from the curse soon after they were born as mortals.'

The king clutched his head in despair. 'Oh … if only I had kept quiet!'

Ganga smiled and shook her head. 'It was meant to be this way. The Vasus asked me if I would agree to be their mother and free them from the curse and I agreed. However, Vashishtha had ruled that the eighth Vasu Prabhasa, the one who actually stole the cow, would have to spend his whole life as a human being. It is he whom I hold in my arms now. Dear husband, this child is destined to attain great fame and will perform many heroic deeds.' She looked down fondly at the baby. 'And now … I'm sorry to part from you, but I have to go …'

'Do not leave me, Ganga!' the king begged. 'How will I live without you?'

'I do not have a choice,' the goddess replied sadly. 'I do not belong to the earth. I, too, am here because of a curse.' She paused, as if reliving a memory, and drew a deep breath. 'In a previous birth, you were King Mahabhishak. You were visiting Indra's court and when we set eyes on one another, we fell in love. Angered, the gods cursed me to live on earth as the wife of a mortal, thus making it possible for us to be together for some years. I was very happy with you, Shantanu, but our time together is over. I will take this baby with me for now, but will return him to you at the proper time.'

Holding the baby, Ganga plunged into the river and disappeared. King Shantanu watched helplessly. Overcome with despair that he would never see his beloved Ganga again, he sat on the bank of the

river for a while, recalling the joy of their life together. Then with leaden steps, he made his way back to the palace. Life seemed to have lost all meaning for him. But he was deeply conscious of his duties to his subjects. He threw himself into the task of governing his kingdom as best as he could and waited for the day when Ganga would send his son back to him.

Shantanu gave up hunting and violence of any kind. He made no attempt to wage war and conquer other territories. However, because of his virtuous behaviour, his kingdom prospered and his power and influence grew rapidly.

One day, as he was strolling along the river, lost in the memories of the happy life he had led with Ganga, he noticed that the waters seemed to have receded. As he looked around to find the cause, he observed that a dam of arrows was impeding the flow of the river. A handsome young boy stood next to it. When Shantanu tried to remove one arrow from the dam, Ganga suddenly appeared.

'This is your son, Devavrata,' she said. 'The time has come for you to be reunited with him. I have brought him up and provided him with the kind of education suitable for a prince. He has been taught the scriptures by none other than Sage Vashishtha, while the mighty Parshurama has trained him in the art of warfare. Take him back with you, Shantanu. As I told you earlier, he is blessed with an extraordinary destiny.'

The king was overjoyed to find his son again, though he was sad that it was not possible for Ganga to live with them. He returned to his palace with his son and life took on a new meaning for him.

As Devavrata grew older, he acquired a reputation for righteousness and for his outstanding skills in the martial arts.

In the course of time, his father Shantanu fell in love with the fisher maiden Satyavati and wanted to marry her. However, her father Dusharaj set a condition – he would allow the king to wed his daughter only if he guaranteed that Satyavati's sons would inherit his throne.

When he observed that his father was pining for Satyavati, Devavrata decided to renounce his rights as the eldest son and heir and thus fulfill the fisherman's condition. When Dusharaj argued that Devavrata's sons might put in a claim for the throne later, he went to the extent of making a vow never to marry, so that Shantanu could find happiness with Satyavati.

This act of sacrifice impressed the gods so much that they showered flowers on him amid cries of 'Bhishma', 'Bhishma'.

From then on, Devavrata came to be known as Bhishma or someone who has made an extremely difficult promise.

Satyavati gave birth to two sons – Chitrangada and Vichitravirya. Chitrangada died childless and Vichitravirya ascended the throne. He had two sons: Dhritirashtra, born of the princess Ambika, and Pandu, born of her sister Ambalika. Dhritirashtra was blind. He and his wife Gandhari gave birth to a hundred sons who became known as the Kauravas. Pandu's five sons, born of Kunti, were known as the Pandavas.

Bhishma played a crucial role in the Mahabharata as the revered elder of both the Pandavas and the Kauravas.

A Tutor for the Princes of Hastinapur

It was a pleasant spring day and the five sons of King Pandu of Hastinapur and his queen Kunti were playing with a ball, just outside the city.

The five of them—Yudhishthira, Bhima, Arjuna, Nakula and Sahadeva—tossed the ball to each other turn by turn.

'Catch, Yudhishthira!' Bhima cried. His older brother leapt to catch it. But the energetic Bhima had thrown too hard. The ball described a wide arc and headed towards a nearby well.

Yudhishthira ran towards the well, extending his arm to catch the ball. But despite his best efforts, the ball escaped his grasp and landed in the water. And then, to his dismay, he realized that his gold ring had slipped off his finger too!

'The ball! It's gone!' Arjuna cried, as his brothers dashed towards the well.

'My ring too,' Yudhishthira said gloomily.

The boys gathered around the edge of the well and peered into it. 'There it is, gleaming in the water!' Nakula pointed to the ring, visible in the water.

'And there's the ball, bobbing next to it!' Sahadeva exclaimed. 'How are we going to get them out?'

The boys glanced at each other, confused and disappointed. 'It's your fault. You threw too hard,' Yudhishthira accused Bhima.

'You weren't quick enough,' Bhima retorted. 'Now our game's been ruined. What will we play with?'

Then they noticed that a man was standing there watching them. A slim, dark-skinned brahmin, with a half-smile on his face. Unusually for a brahmin, he was armed with a bow and arrow. 'You are the princes of Hastinapur, aren't you?' he remarked. 'The descendants of King Bharata. Surely you have been taught the use of a bow and arrow? Why don't you use your skill to extract the ball from the well?'

'Extract the ball with a bow and arrow?' Yudhishthira replied. 'Is that possible? If you can do it, kind sir, we would be happy to reward you with a meal at the house of our guru Kripacharya.'

The stranger laughed. 'Never mind about the meal, but I will help you.'

He plucked a blade of grass and, after muttering a mantra, flung it with force into the well where it pierced the ball. He followed this with more blades of grass till he had formed a chain long enough to pull out the ball.

The five Pandavas watched him with great excitement. They clapped their hands with glee when he took out the ball and gave it to them.

'You are a magician, sir!' Yudhishthira exclaimed. 'Please take out my ring too, if you can.'

'Definitely,' said the man. 'It's quite easy to do that.' He removed the bow he was carrying from his shoulder and fitted an arrow into it. As the boys watched, the arrow sprang into the water and landed right in the middle of the ring. There was such power in his shot that the arrow rebounded with great force, carrying the ring back with it.

'Here's your ring, prince.' The man handed the ring to Yudhishthira with an amused smile.

The five boys were so awestruck that they could not speak for a moment. Then they folded their hands and bowed low. 'Who are you, respected sir?' Yudhishthira asked hesitantly. 'We have never seen such feats of skill.'

'Go and inform your grandfather Bhishma about these feats,' the man replied. 'He will tell you who I am.'

The Pandavas rushed back to the palace and looked for Bhishma. Full of excitement, they narrated the whole incident to him.

When he had heard the whole story, Bhishma nodded and said thoughtfully, 'It can be none other than Drona. He is the son of the great sage Bhardwaj and husband to Kripi, your guru Kripacharya's sister. The accomplished warrior Parashuram himself has trained him in the use of weapons. No wonder that he could perform such an extraordinary deed.' Bhishma paused as if reflecting on what had happened. 'Drona has arrived at the right time,' he said finally. 'I was looking for a tutor who could further hone your skills in the martial arts. Let us go and invite him into the palace.'

The Pandavas accompanied their grandfather happily to find Drona. Bhishma greeted Drona with great respect and offered him the job of tutor to the princes. Drona accepted at once.

Drona was indeed in much need of a job. He had followed the usual course of education at his father's ashram and acquired great skill in archery. After completing his studies, he had married Kripi. In due course, they were blessed with a son whom they named Ashwatthama.

Drona, however, was not able to earn much, despite the extent of his knowledge. Eager to keep his family in comfort, he told Kripi, 'I hear that the great sage Parashuram is distributing his wealth among brahmins before he retires to the forest. Let me go and meet him. Then maybe we will be able to provide nourishing food for our son.'

When Drona reached Parashuram's ashram, however, he was dismayed to find that he was too late.

'I am sorry, son,' Parashuram said ruefully. 'I have given away all that I owned. Now all I have left to offer you is my knowledge.'

'There can be no greater wealth than that,' Drona replied, bowing low. Parashuram's expertise in the use of weapons was legendary. There was no one equal to him in the three worlds, it was said.

Drona was already renowned for his skill as an archer. Once he had completed his training under Parashuram, he became the unrivalled master of the military arts. This was a highly valued accomplishment and Drona felt he would be able to find employment with any ruler.

However, when he returned to meet his wife and son before he set off to search for a job, he found that conditions had deteriorated further at home.

In tears, Kripi narrated an incident. 'Ashwatthama came and asked me if he could have some milk,' she said. '"What is this wonderful drink, ma?" he asked. "My friends say it is white in colour and delicious in taste. It has excellent qualities too – it makes boys healthy and strong.

Can you give me some?" I didn't know what to do!' Kripi wept. 'How could I tell him we could not afford to buy milk?'

Highly mortified that he could not provide for his family, Drona said, 'Do not worry, Kripi. I will approach my good friend King Drupada of Panchala for help. He studied at my father's ashram and we were like brothers. In fact, he often used to say that he would share half his kingdom with me when he ascended the throne. He is sure to come to our aid.'

Drona immediately headed for the court of Panchala. When he arrived there and greeted the king, to his dismay, Drupada did not appear to recognize him. To remind him, Drona said, 'Noble king, don't you remember that we were close friends in the days of our boyhood? We studied together at my father Sage Bharadwaj's ashram. You were so attached to me then that you even offered to share whatever you owned with me. I am not interested in your wealth, but I hope you will keep me with you in your court.'

How could Drona guess that his friend had changed since then and had become arrogant and proud of his status and of his wealth and power as a king? When Drupada laughed mockingly at him, Drona was stunned.

'O brahmin,' Drupada said, 'you claim to be my friend. Don't you know that friendship can only exist among equals? How can a beggarly brahmin like you claim friendship with a king who is seated on his throne? Go your way and don't come back ever again to make such nonsensical demands on me.'

Drona turned on his heel and left, numb with humiliation. Utterly cast down, he decided to go and visit his brother-in-law Kripacharya in Hastinapur and see if he could help him find a job. The thought of taking revenge on Drupada for the insult was also burning a hole in his heart. One day, he would bring about the downfall of his haughty friend, he vowed.

When Drona was appointed to the job of training the young princes of Hastinapur in the use of weapons, a plan began to take shape in his mind. He threw himself heart and soul into moulding not just the Pandavas but also their cousins, the hundred Kauravas, into accomplished warriors. He imparted the same lessons to his son Ashwatthama as well, and in a few years' time he had groomed his pupils to such a level that they were good enough to take on any force in the world. Arjuna, who possessed great powers of concentration, turned out to be the most skilled archer among them and was his guru's favourite.

One day, Drona decided to test the young princes on the level of their expertise. While he was bathing in the river Ganga, suddenly, a crocodile caught hold of his leg. Drona could have saved himself with ease but instead he cried out as if in panic, 'Help! Save me, my boys! Save me!'

Arjuna was the first to react. Without a moment's hesitation, he shot several arrows into the crocodile's body and killed it. Drona emerged from the river, exulting in his student's skill. He embraced Arjuna and praised him wholeheartedly, saying, 'My prince, you have proved yourself a worthy pupil. This is exactly what I expected from you.'

The time had come to take revenge on Drupada, he thought. His students were such intrepid warriors that no force would be able to withstand them. First, Drona decided to send Duryodhana and the Kauravas.

'My boys,' he said, 'I have spent many years trying to groom you into perfect warriors. Now the time has come to prove your mettle and pay my gurudakshina – my fees as your teacher. Go and bring back the arrogant King Drupada of Panchala in chains. Only then will I be convinced that you have absorbed all my teachings well.'

Duryodhana and his brothers armed themselves and mounted their horses. They galloped off, eager to prove themselves. King Drupada was surprised when he received the news that the Kauravas were advancing towards Panchala with a large army. He had no enmity with the kingdom of Hastinapur. All the same, he prepared for battle.

The Pandavas stayed back at a short distance, since their guru had charged Duryodhana with this responsibility. They were aware, however, that Drupada was no minor warrior.

'We will step in if they fail,' Arjuna said to his brothers.

A furious battle began when the two armies came face to face. After some time, it became obvious that the Kauravas were no match for the doughty Drupada. Far from capturing him, they were compelled to flee for their lives. Seeing his cousins in retreat, Arjuna leapt on to his chariot. Exhorting Yudhishthira to stay back, he charged at Drupada with his three other brothers beside him. Bhima was a formidable sight as he advanced, armed with his mighty mace, with Nakula and Sahadeva guiding the chariot. They headed straight towards Drupada, ignoring all the other soldiers. When they were close, Arjuna let loose such a dense shower of arrows that Drupada got confused. He felt as if darkness had descended on him. Arjuna dived into the king's chariot and seized him. Then he bundled him into his own chariot and sped away. When they saw that their king had been made prisoner, his army surrendered.

When the captive king was brought before Drona, the brahmin addressed him calmly. 'Do not fear that you will lose your life, great king,' he said. 'We were friends in our boyhood, but when I came to you for help, you insulted me. You said friendship was only possible among equals – only a king could be friends with a king. Today I have conquered your kingdom and am in a superior position to you. But I will be magnanimous. I will return half of your kingdom to you so that we become equals.'

Drona marked out which portion of Panchala would be his and set Drupada free. He believed that he had behaved honourably, but little did he realize that he had created a mortal enemy.

It was Drupada who now burned with the desire for revenge, and devoted his life to accomplishing it. He performed rigorous penances and sacrifices, praying to the gods to grant him a son who would be a warrior mighty enough to slay Drona and a daughter who would marry the brilliant archer Arjuna. Finally, his efforts were rewarded and a son, Drishtadyumna, and a daughter, Draupadi, were born out of the sacrificial fire. Drishtadyumna would later defeat and kill Drona in the battle of the Mahabharata and Draupadi would go on to marry the Pandavas.

The Palace of Lac

Dhritirashtra, the father of the Kauravas, was the older brother but, being blind, he could not ascend the throne of Hastinapur. His younger brother Pandu ruled as king and being an indomitable warrior, he greatly expanded the kingdom. However, because of a curse, Pandu died early and then Dhritirashtra took on the reins of government.

The five Pandavas and the hundred Kauravas had grown into young men by this time. Yudhishthira was the oldest among them, so he was anointed the crown prince. Within a year, he had won the hearts of the people because of his gentle manner and righteous conduct. As if this were not enough, Bhima was admired because of his superhuman strength and Arjuna for his valour and skills in archery. In this way, the popularity of the Pandavas continued to grow and their cousins, the Kauravas, became extremely jealous of them.

Matters came to a head when Duryodhana, the eldest among the Kauravas, heard from his spies that the popular sentiment was that Yudhishthira should be crowned king. Burning with resentment, he approached his father when Dhritirashtra was alone and said, 'Pitashri, why did you anoint Yudhishthira as crown prince? Now our subjects are eager that he occupy the throne of Hastinapur. You have trampled on the hopes of your own sons by this action.'

'My son,' Dhritirashtra replied gently, 'try and understand. I am following the right course of action. It was my brother Pandu who built up this vast kingdom and it would only be just to let his eldest son succeed. It will be in your best interest to support your cousin. Apart from the common people, our highly respected elders Bhishma, Drona, Kripa and my half-brother Vidura all think highly of the Pandavas. Do not let your hatred cloud your judgement.'

'Pitashri, you overestimate the opinion of our subjects,' Duryodhana replied. 'Besides, you know our grandfather Bhishma will never take sides. If you send the Pandavas away for some time, everyone will forget them and I can win the public over to favour me as the next ruler. Why don't you send them away to a place like Varanavata for a year?'

Like any father, even while conscious of his duties towards his dead brother's children, Dhritirashtra was more partial to his own sons. Duryodhana well knew this and began to hatch a plot to get rid of his cousins. His villainous maternal uncle Shakuni was his main adviser in this matter.

When their plans had been finalized, Shakuni's minister Kanika approached Dhritirashtra. 'Your majesty,' he said, 'as your well-wisher, I would advise you to look out for your own interests and those of your sons. You are letting the Pandavas thrive in your kingdom. Soon, they will grow so strong that the future of your own family will be in peril. Please accept my humble advice and send them away from Hastinapur.'

After thinking over the matter for some time, Dhritirashtra sent for Yudhishthira. 'My son,' he said, embracing the prince with a false show of affection, 'you know how much I care for you and your brothers.'

'Indeed, uncle, you have never let us feel we are fatherless,' Yudhishthira replied. 'You are more affectionate towards us than even your own sons.'

Hearing this, Dhritirashtra smiled inwardly. 'Do you know about this beautiful place called Varanavata?' he asked. 'A famous shrine is located there, dedicated to Lord Shiva. I want you to go and live there for a year with your brothers. You will earn much merit by worshipping there.'

Yudhishthira immediately guessed that his uncle was trying to get him and his brothers out of the way. However, he had no reasons to offer for refusing, especially when his uncle said that he was providing them with an opportunity to gain merit through religious activities. So, with a heavy heart, he agreed respectfully.

When he heard that the Pandavas had decided to go to Varanavata, there was no one more delighted than Duryodhana. While his cousins were preparing for their departure along with their mother Kunti, he sent for Purochana, a minister in his father's court. 'You know how much I value your services, dear Purochana,' he said. 'With my cousins out of the way, the path has been cleared for me to ascend the throne of Hastinapur. If you do as I say, I will reward you with enormous wealth.'

'How can I refuse you anything, your highness?' Purochana replied obsequiously. 'Just tell me what you require from me.'

'Make haste and go to Varanavata,' Duryodhana commanded. 'You must build a fabulous palace there for my cousins, the Pandavas. It should be most luxurious to look at, but you must use the most inflammable materials in the construction – materials like lac and wax.'

'I will go immediately, your highness, and build this palace,' Purochana said with a bow.

'Wait, I am not done,' Duryodhana said. 'The palace has to be ready by the time my cousins reach the city. You must also store pots of oil and ghee in it and perfume it heavily so that they smell no other odours. Once they reach Varanavata, invite them to stay at this palace. At an appropriate time, set fire to the building and make it look like an accident.'

'Your wish is my command,' Purochana replied. 'May I take your leave now?'

Duryodhana nodded and the minister set off post-haste to execute his evil mission.

When the news that the Pandavas were to leave Hastinapur spread through the city, all the people were first astonished, then grief-stricken. A group of them approached Yudhishthira saying, 'Dear prince, why are you going? You know how much we all love you. Please do not abandon us.'

'My friends, your love warms my heart,' Yudhishthira replied sadly. 'But I cannot disobey my uncle's orders. He is like a father to me.'

Disappointed, the group left. Soon, the time to leave came and the citizens of Hastinapur bade the Pandavas a tearful farewell. Their uncle Vidura walked with them for some distance. Using a dialect few people could understand, he told Yudhishthira, 'My son, I wish you a safe stay in Varanavata, but please remember a few things. Princes are always under threat. You are highly intelligent and will grasp what I mean. Remember, a wise man finds ways to protect himself and his family against weapons that are more dangerous than swords and arrows, weapons like fire and poison.'

Yudhishthira sighed. 'Uncle, you have always given good advice. I will remember your words.'

Vidura, however, was not done giving advice. 'How does a rat protect itself in winter? By digging a hole,' he continued. 'A clever man will use this method against fire. After this is done, the way ahead will become clear. The stars are there to guide you, my son.'

Yudhishthira murmured his thanks to his uncle and they took their leave of the wise and kind Vidura.

'What was Vidura saying?' Kunti asked after a while.

'He was warning me against danger,' Yudhishthira replied. 'Our respected elder uncle and noble cousins do not dare to face us openly. They are planning to use underhand means to destroy us.'

This added to the gloom that had possessed the five brothers ever since they left Hastinapur.

A lavish welcome awaited them in Varanavata, however. Apart from being sacred to Lord Shiva, this city had great significance because the righteous Raja Harishchandra lived there during the period of his misfortune. The citizens had decorated the streets to honour the Pandavas. Prominent men hosted them for the next ten days. On the tenth day, Purochana invited them to occupy the palace of lac.

'Your loving uncle, King Dhritirashtra himself instructed me to build this beautiful palace for you, so that you may be comfortable here,' he said with a low bow. 'Please come and enjoy its luxuries.'

When they approached the palace, the Pandavas noticed that a moat had been dug around it.

'See what pains your uncle has taken for your protection,' Purochana pointed out. 'He instructed me to build a moat to guard you against intruders.'

The real reason, of course, was to prevent them from escaping.

After the minister left, Yudhishthira drew Bhima aside. 'Can you smell something strange?' he asked. 'I think this house is built of highly inflammable materials. Our uncle Vidura warned me against fire. No doubt he overheard them plotting.'

Bhima became furious. 'So this was their plan? Let us not invite death by staying here,' he said. 'Did you notice the moat around the palace? We will be trapped like rats. We should go back to the house we were staying in till now.'

'I think they will not set fire to the house immediately or their game will be exposed,' Yudhishthira replied. 'I am sure uncle Vidura has made some plans to help us escape.'

So, the Pandavas decided to wait and watch. It was an unnerving time, but Yudhishthira was convinced that they would be able to foil Duryodhana's plans.

A few days later, a strange man approached the palace of lac saying that he wished to meet Yudhishthira. The prince invited him in. Using the same dialect that Vidura had used, the man repeated their uncle's words. Immediately Yudhishthira guessed that he was a person he could trust.

'I have been sent by your uncle to help you,' the man continued. 'I am a miner by profession. I have been instructed to build a tunnel underground to create a secret path to the banks of the Ganga from this palace.'

'I am extremely relieved to hear this,' Yudhishthira said. 'But this is not a simple task. It will have to be completed in great secrecy. That villainous Purochana never leaves our side. Anyway, I will try to entice him away from the house, so you can perform your task.'

The Pandavas decided to while away time roaming in the forests surrounding the city. Actually, there was a purpose behind this innocuous activity. By spending time in the forests, they could familiarize themselves with the lay of the land and keep Purochana from suspecting that something else was afoot in the house. They made frequent hunting trips and Purochana clung to them like a leech wherever they went.

Almost a year went by in this manner. And by then, the tunnel was complete. It had a narrow opening, just broad enough for one person to enter, which the Pandavas covered with a rug. After the entry point, however, the miner had made the tunnel wide enough so they could walk through it comfortably.

'My work here is complete,' the miner informed Yudhishthira. 'But the fateful day approaches. I have been told that Purochana plans to set fire to the palace on the fourteenth day of the dark fortnight – the darkest day of the month. You have to be extra vigilant that night.'

'I am extremely grateful to you for your help, my good man,' Yudhishthira said. 'You have saved our lives.' He rewarded the miner handsomely, and sent him on his way.

Then Yudhishthira immediately called his mother and brothers. 'It is time to escape,' he whispered. 'But we have to make sure that Purochana does not suspect anything.'

Kunti was quick to reply. 'I will organize a feast tomorrow and feed the poor of the city. And we will ply Purochana with liquor so that he falls into a deep sleep. Then we can set the palace on fire and escape.'

Purochana was delighted to hear about the feast. It confirmed his belief that the Pandavas had no inkling of what lay in store for them.

Kunti summoned cooks and other attendants to prepare a lavish banquet. She sent for a crier to announce the invitation through the town. It caused great excitement. In the evening, a large number of people turned up to attend the feast and enjoyed all kinds of delicacies to their heart's content. A complacent Purochana consumed a large amount of liquor, thinking of the reward that he would receive from Duryodhana. After he had fallen into a drunken stupor, Kunti and four of her sons entered the tunnel one by one. Bhima stayed behind. He had taken on the task of setting the fire himself. Once the others had slipped into the tunnel, he ran swiftly through the palace of lac with a torch, touching the walls, the furniture and the lavish furnishings with its flame. Then he swiftly lowered himself into the tunnel, even as flames were flaring up through the palace of lac.

The crackling of the fire awoke the people of Varanavata. When they rushed out of their houses to see what was happening, they were horrified at the sight of the blazing palace. They heard fearful sounds of the roof and walls crashing down. But despite many attempts, it was impossible to go close enough to douse the flames and rescue the princes whom they believed were trapped inside. There was no way that anyone could cross the moat fast enough. As they watched helplessly, the suspicion that King Dhritirashtra and his sons could be behind the fire crossed many people's minds.

Little did they know that the Pandavas were making good their escape. Worried that the tunnel might cave in before they got out, the mighty Bhima hoisted his mother on his back, the twins Nakula and Sahadeva on his hips and Yudhishthira and Arjuna on his back to be able to move as fast as possible.

When they emerged on the banks of the Ganga, they found a man waiting for them. He greeted them politely. 'I have been keeping watch here for several nights on your uncle Vidura's instructions,' he said. 'He ordered me to provide help whenever you found the opportunity to escape. Come, I have a boat waiting. We must not lose any time.'

The man spoke in the same dialect that Vidura had used. This convinced Yudhishthira of his sincerity. 'Let's hurry, mother,' he told Kunti. 'We must get away before anyone suspects that we survived.'

Kunti and her sons stopped into the boat and the boatman plied his oars vigorously to take them across the river. Soon, they had reached the other shore.

'How can I thank you enough for your help?' Kunti said to the boatman as they stepped on to the bank. 'We will always be in your debt for saving our lives.'

'This opportunity to serve you is the greatest honour I could receive, your majesty,' the boatman replied. 'I consider myself fortunate indeed. The noble Vidura has compensated me generously. He told me to advise you to take the path that leads south and follow the stars for guidance. You are to keep your identity secret for the next few months.'

Kunti and her sons entered the dark forest without wasting any time. They walked as fast as they could to put some distance between themselves and the cursed town of Varanavata.

When the fire died down, the people of the town managed to get across the moat and examine the remains of the magnificent palace. They found seven bodies there. One was that of Purochana. They assumed that the other six were those of the five Pandavas and their mother. Actually, they were those of a woman who belonged to the nishada tribe and her five sons who had gone off to sleep in the palace after the feast.

When the news reached Hastinapur, Dhritirashtra pretended to be cast down with sorrow. Duryodhana exulted secretly that his plan had been so successful. Bhishma, however, was overcome with grief. The funeral rites for the Pandavas were conducted according to custom. After the ceremonies were complete, Vidura took the stricken Bhishma aside.

'Please wipe your tears, sire,' he said. 'This is for your ears alone. The Pandavas are alive. They survived the plot hatched by Prince Duryodhana and Shakuni to burn them in the palace of lac. At present, they are living in disguise. But when the time is right, they will return.'

'I cannot find the words to express my relief,' Bhishma said with a deep sigh. 'If only your brother were as righteous and wise as you, dear Vidura.'

Dhritirashtra and his sons believed that with the Pandavas gone, there were no obstacles in their path. They had no inkling that the brothers were alive and well and living in the dense forest of Siddhivana.

Draupadi's Swayamvara

The Pandavas were leading secluded lives in the forest of Siddhivana. Soon after they arrived there, Bhima married a rakshasi named Hidimbi, who had been of great help to them. Hidimbi took the Pandavas to a sacred lake called Salivahana and built a cottage for them there. Seven peaceful months went by in this pleasant place.

Then one morning, Yudhishthira noticed an elderly sage coming their way. He rose immediately to pay his respects, then realized it was Vyasa himself.

Vyasa accepted their greetings and blessed them affectionately. He spent a long time with them and had comforting words for each member of the Pandava family. 'Do not despair, Kunti,' he said. 'These days of suffering will soon pass. There is good news in store. Your daughter-in-law Hidimbi will give birth to a son who will be ever-famous for his heroic deeds.'

'You are all-knowing, sire,' Bhima folded his hands and bowed gratefully to the sage. 'But how long are we to stay here?' he asked. 'When will our kingdom be restored to us?'

'Wait for your son to be born,' Vyasa replied. 'Then dress yourself in bark and deerskin and go to the city of Ekachakra.'

Seven more months went by and Bhima's son Ghatotkacha was born. The baby was a source of great delight to all of them. However, the time to move on had come.

Hidimbi shed bitter tears, but Bhima could not disregard Vyasa's advice. So, they set off for Ekachakra, dressed as ascetics, with matted hair and garments of bark.

A brahmin gave them shelter and they began to support themselves by begging for alms. And then, they heard something intriguing – that King Drupada of Panchala was holding a grand swayamvara for his daughter Draupadi in the city of Kampilya.

When the news spread, many brahmins decided to head there, knowing that the king would be distributing generous gifts. The Pandavas decided to accompany them and see what fate had in store for them.

Princess Draupadi was renowned for her incomparable beauty. Drupada was known to be a powerful ruler too. Consequently, kings and princes from all over the country arrived in Kampilya to vie for her hand. Thus, when the day of the swayamvara arrived, the beautifully decorated hall of Drupada's place was crowded with powerful monarchs and warriors. The Pandavas entered quietly and decided to sit with the brahmins and observe the proceedings incognito.

Drupada had personally experienced Arjuna's skill in archery. He had already performed rigorous penances because he longed to marry his daughter to Arjuna. For this reason, he had created a test which only a man with skills equal to those of the legendary archer could pass. The fact was that the news of the Pandavas' death in the palace of lac had spread far and wide, but Drupada clung to the hope that the five brothers might have escaped.

When all the suitors were assembled, and had occupied their seats, Draupadi's brother Drishtadyumna led his sister into the hall. Dressed in gorgeous garments of silk and brocade and decked with golden ornaments, the princess looked more beautiful than ever. After mantras had been chanted for an auspicious beginning, Drishtadyumna rose to his feet and addressed the assembly.

'Welcome, noble princes, to our mighty kingdom of Panchala and to the swayamvara of my lovely and accomplished sister. I thank you for honouring us with your gracious presence at this important event. You well know that my sister Draupadi is one of a kind – not only a great beauty but a woman possessing extraordinary intelligence, who is also well-versed in all the arts. She will marry only a man equal to her – one who possesses the greatest expertise in the martial arts as well as valour far above the ordinary.' He paused to look around, while the assembled rulers twirled their moustaches, each trying to stare the other down. 'I request all the suitors to kindly listen carefully while I explain the conditions of the test that we have devised to select a suitable bridegroom for Draupadi. This stringent test will determine which of you fits our standards.'

The princes leaned forward eagerly, as Drishtadyumna continued, pointing to an enormous bow. 'You are to lift this bow, known as Kindhura, and string it. You can see the target placed above, a fish hanging on a revolving wheel, tied to a pole. Your task is to shoot an arrow into the eye of the fish. But ... you cannot look at it directly – you have to watch its reflection in a pan of oil set below it. This test, my friends, has been created with great thought as the true assessment of a proficient archer.'

The suitors shrugged and smiled as if it were a simple task. Then Drishtadyumna turned to Draupadi. 'Dear sister, I am sure you would like to know who are the mighty warriors aspiring to win your hand. Let me introduce them.' Drishtadyumna then proceeded to name all the powerful rulers who had gathered there. Among them were Duryodhana and his brothers, his friend Karna, his uncle Shakuni with his sons, Drona's son Ashwatthama, Salya and Jayadratha among many others. Krishna and Balarama were there too, along with others from the Vrishni clan.

The trumpets were blown, King Drupada gave the signal, and the contest began. One by one, the kings and princes came forward with great confidence. But when they tried to lift the bow, most found they could not raise it even an inch, let alone string it. Some managed to lift it but were unequal to the task of stringing it. King after mighty king retired crestfallen and disheartened. Murmurs of discontent were spreading through the hall when it came to Karna's turn. Exclamations of surprise resounded as he lifted the bow effortlessly, then bent and strung it with ease. He was about to take a shot at the target when Draupadi's voice rang out: 'I am a kshatriya princess, I cannot marry the lowborn son of a charioteer.'

A stunned silence descended on the hall. Humiliated, Karna flung down the bow and stalked out of the court. Duryodhana started up to follow his friend but his uncle restrained him.

The next prince in line leapt forward eagerly, but he failed to lift the bow. And soon all the highborn suitors had tried their hand at stringing the bow and failed.

King Drupada looked around at all the prospective bridegrooms, who sat there sullen and disgruntled. He cried out in despair, 'Is there no man worthy of my daughter here? Have we stopped producing warriors?'

When he heard this, Arjuna sprang to his feet. 'Let me try my hand,' he replied.

'A brahmin?' Mocking laughter filled the hall. 'He thinks he can succeed when the best kshatriya warriors have failed?'

'Why not?' Drishtadyumna's voice rang out. 'Anyone capable can try.'

Arjuna approached the bow. He circled it reverently then prostrated himself before it. Then he reached out and picked it up effortlessly. In one graceful movement, he had strung Kindhura. And even before the astonished kings could react, he had shot an arrow straight into the fish's eye.

Cries of amazement filled the hall and conches and drum beats proclaimed his victory. A joyful Draupadi approached Arjuna with a garland of flowers and placed it around his neck.

But the defeated kings could not tolerate this. They erupted in cries of protest. 'Drupada has insulted us!' 'How can he give his daughter to a brahmin?'

Within minutes, there was mayhem as the disgruntled suitors drew their weapons and the clash of swords drowned out all other sounds. Soon, the battle spread out onto the palace grounds and became an opportunity for the Pandavas to prove their mettle.

Frustrated that they had been outdone, the Kauravas launched a furious attack on Arjuna. But they had not reckoned with Bhima's extraordinary strength. Swiftly he uprooted a tree and stood by his brother to beat off anyone who came close. The Pandavas fought with all their might and in a short time they had routed Duryodhana and his supporters. Seeing this, the other hostile princes fell back.

Then Krishna spoke. 'This brahmin has won the hand of the princess in a fair contest. Her brother himself proclaimed that all were free to participate. There should be no more fighting.'

The affronted princes immediately called for their chariots and a stream of disappointed suitors departed Drupada's palace without any ceremony. No polite greetings were exchanged as they left, but everyone was buzzing with curiosity about this unusual brahmin who was so adept at archery.

Once all the rejected suitors had gone, the Pandavas set off for the potter's house along with Draupadi. Full of excitement, they called out, 'Ma, look what we have brought for you.' Kunti called out from inside without looking, 'Whatever it is, remember to share it!'

The five brothers did not know what to say in reply and stood there exchanging worried glances. When Kunti appeared at the door, Yudhishthira said in a low voice, 'Ma, Arjuna has won the hand of this lovely girl in a contest of skill. She is Draupadi, the daughter of King Drupada of Panchala.'

Kunti was stunned. She recalled her impetuous words, but recovered her composure to welcome Draupadi in.

Later, she took Yudhishthira aside and said, 'My son, I did not realize what I was saying. But now that I have spoken, how can I take back my words? What are we to do?'

'Do not worry, ma,' Yudhishthira replied. 'Arjuna won a bride for himself and he will marry her.'

However, Arjuna hesitated. 'How can I go against my mother's directive?' he said. 'Draupadi will have to marry all of us.'

Krishna and Balarama had followed them to the house of the potter. Krishna bent to touch the feet of his aunt Kunti and Balarama too introduced himself.

'I'm overjoyed to see that you managed to escape the deadly palace of lac,' Krishna said. 'But please be careful. Do not reveal your true identity as yet.'

After some more conversation, Krishna and Balarama left.

However, one other person had followed the Pandavas when they left King Drupada's palace with Draupadi. It was her brother Drishtadyumna.

Drupada had been in despair ever since the unknown brahmin won Draupadi's hand. His greatest wish had been to see his daughter married to Arjuna and he had designed the contest in a manner that none but the most accomplished archer in the land could win.

'My son,' he said to Drishtadyumna, 'my heart is about to burst with grief. I had hoped that Arjuna would appear to compete and Draupadi would be married to a warrior of his stature. And now she has been thrown away on this unknown brahmin. He is a good archer, no doubt, but what kind of a life has my lovely daughter been condemned to?'

'Pitashri, please do not lose heart like this,' Drishtadyumna comforted his father. 'There was something about that man's bearing that tells me he is no ordinary brahmin. And what courage he and his brothers displayed! They beat back the combined force of the doughtiest warriors in the country. I will follow them and keep watch to find out how our Draupadi is faring.'

So, the prince of Panchala made his way to the potter's house too, making sure to keep a safe distance. When he saw Krishna and Balarama visiting, his curiosity deepened. 'They have to be the Pandavas,' he said to himself. 'Why would Krishna go to meet an ordinary brahmin?'

After a while, when he saw the five brothers set out to beg for alms, according to their custom, he became more than a little disturbed. But when he saw the contented look on Draupadi's face as she distributed the food, and then sat down to eat, he heaved a sigh of relief. Night was falling, so Drishtadyumna felt it was safe now to creep a little closer to the house so that he could eavesdrop on their conversation. To his astonishment, he found the brothers talking about weapons and warfare rather than religious ceremonies and mantras. No brahmin family would be discussing such matters, he well knew.

Reassured and delighted, he hurried back to the palace to share the good news with his father. 'Pitashri, we have no cause to be concerned about Draupadi's future,' he told King Drupada enthusiastically. 'I am convinced that these brahmins are none other than the Pandavas in disguise. There was an elderly lady they addressed as mother, who must be Kunti. The young man who won the archery contest has to be Arjuna – no one else possesses such skills. The powerfully built brother who uprooted the tree is Bhima, I'm sure; the one who defeated Duryodhana in the fight must be Yudhishthira; and the other two brave warriors Nakula and Sahadeva.'

The dark shadows cleared from Drupada's face at once. 'Son, you have lifted a great weight from my heart!' he exclaimed, embracing his son. 'We must prepare for a grand wedding ceremony for your sister.'

Drupada wasted no time. When dawn broke the next day, he immediately dispatched some priests along with attendants bearing rich garments and other lavish gifts for Kunti and her sons along with an invitation to come to the palace so that the wedding could be performed in style. He sent beautifully decorated chariots to carry them.

When the so-called brahmins arrived, their demeanour made it clear that they were quite accustomed to this royal treatment.

After greeting them warmly, Drupada began, 'It gives me great pleasure to welcome such accomplished warriors and their noble mother to my palace.' Then he turned to Arjuna and said, 'Young man, you are indeed one of the greatest archers I have seen. I cannot describe how delighted I am that you will be my daughter's husband. However, there is one question that bothers me. Please could you tell us something about your background? Who were your ancestors? Where do you come from? As a father, I am anxious to know what kind of family my daughter is marrying into.'

Hearing this, Yudhishthira got to his feet and addressed the king, 'Your majesty, I fully appreciate your concern. But please rest assured, your daughter is marrying into one of the noblest families in the country. We are the sons of King Pandu of Hastinapur.' Then he introduced his mother and his four brothers to Drupada.

Drupada was almost speechless with joy. 'My fondest dreams have come true. I could not have hoped for a better match for my daughter. But please, will you tell us how you escaped the terrible palace of lac? It was rumoured that you had all been burnt alive.'

'Pardon me, Pitashri,' Drishtadyumna interposed. 'Let us proceed with the wedding ceremony first. There will be plenty of time to talk later.'

'You are right,' the king replied quickly. 'Come, Arjuna, it was my life's wish to give my daughter's hand into yours.'

Yudhishthira cleared his throat and said, 'Sire, according to my mother's wish, your daughter has to marry all five of us. I am the eldest, so I will go first.'

'What?' the king almost fell from his seat in surprise. 'What kind of sacrilege is this? It is acceptable for a man to marry more than one woman. But it is against our code of morals for a woman to marry more than one man.'

'We are well aware of that, sire,' Yudhishthira replied politely. 'But we five brothers took a vow to share whatever we have with each other. When we returned with Draupadi, our mother reminded us that we must share whatever we had brought home. At that moment, she was inside the house and did not see that we had brought her a daughter-in-law. But the words had left her mouth before she realized what she had said. As dutiful sons, we cannot disobey her. And as for the code of morals, there are instances when a woman has married more than one man, like Sage Jatila's daughter. So, it is not something new or unusual.'

Drupada, however, was still not convinced.

Just then, Sage Vyasa's arrival was announced.

After greetings were exchanged, the issue was placed before Vyasa.

'Respected Vyasa,' King Drupada said, 'You are the most knowledgeable among all on the rules of correct conduct. How can I give my daughter in marriage to five men at the same time? All my peers will condemn me for this sacrilege.'

The sage did not hesitate for a moment before giving his view. 'I am aware of your dilemma, O king,' he said. 'In fact, I came here specially to resolve this matter. It is true that this custom has fallen out of practice in recent times. However, it is perfectly permissible for a woman to marry more than one man. There is nothing immoral about it.'

Once the wise and learned sage had pronounced his opinion, King Drupada did not hesitate any longer. Draupadi was married to the five Pandavas before the sacred fire. A grand celebration followed.

This marriage ensured that the brothers now had a powerful ally. Panchala was an extremely prosperous kingdom and Drupada and Drishtadyumna were well known for their prowess in battle. Krishna and the Vrishnis had also demonstrated their support to the Pandavas. The five brothers were no longer mendicants wandering through the forest. Their position had become very strong.

The Fateful Game of Dice

The news did not take long to spread far and wide. The story that the Pandavas were alive and well, and that Arjuna was the mysterious brahmin who had won Draupadi's hand at the swayamvara, created great excitement everywhere.

After their defeat, Duryodhana and Karna had returned to Hastinapur burning with rage and frustration. When it was confirmed that it was their arch-enemies, the Pandavas, who had humbled them, their fury knew no bounds.

As for Bhishma, he was ecstatic that the Pandavas had survived the terrible palace of lac. When he publicly shared his joy, Dhritirashtra had no choice but to hide his disappointment and even agree to welcome his nephews back to Hastinapur. A discussion took place between the elders of the land, and Bhishma and Drona suggested that it would only be fair to give half the kingdom to the five brothers. Dhritirashtra had to agree, even though Duryodhana and Karna had been pressing him to somehow keep the Pandavas out.

Vidura was sent to the court of Panchala to invite the five brothers back to their homeland. However, it took him some time to convince a suspicious Kunti. Vidura was eventually able to reassure her that her sons would not come to any harm in their hometown.

They entered Hastinapur to find that a grand welcome had been arranged for them. The people had decorated the city with garlands of flowers to celebrate the return of their beloved Pandavas. They beat drums, danced and sang in honour of the safe return of Pandu's sons. Dhritirashtra played his part well, greeting his nephews with false words, 'My sons, it gives me great joy to see you back in the land of your forefathers.' He paused for a moment before continuing. 'However, the sad truth is that my sons will never be able to keep peace with you. Hence, in your best interest it has been decided that we partition the kingdom and you reign over half of it. Why don't you take possession of the ruined city of Khandavaprastha and rebuild it as your capital? It was the place from which our ancestors Pururavas and Yayati ruled. Please restore its ancient glory and earn the blessings of your forefathers.'

The Pandavas accepted this offer and rebuilt the abandoned city, renaming it Indraprastha. Yudhishthira was crowned king and with his wise and righteous rule the kingdom began to prosper. The Pandavas were guided by Krishna and had many other noble allies. Thirty-six years passed by in this manner without any problem. By this time the kingdom had grown in strength and prosperity to the extent that Yudhishthira was advised to perform the Rajasuya yagna. This sacrifice, if successfully completed, would proclaim him to be the most powerful king in the land.

Duryodhana and the other Kauravas, however, could not tolerate this. Duryodhana had never wanted to share the kingdom with his cousins. He had grown more and more resentful as he watched their steady ascent among the rulers of the region. This event, which would celebrate their preeminence, was the last straw.

Yudhishthira completed a successful Rajasuya yagna and numerous illustrious rulers paid homage to him. The result was that Duryodhana's feelings of envy became uncontrollable. The magnificent palace the Pandavas had built, furnished in the most exquisite manner, their lavish lifestyle, the love of their subjects and Draupadi's much-praised beauty, all added fuel to the fire of his hatred.

There was only one thought occupying Duryodhana's mind now – how to destroy his cousins so completely that they could never prosper again. Noticing his preoccupation, his maternal uncle Shakuni asked, 'What's the matter, my son? I see that nothing seems to please you these days. Why do you keep sighing so dolefully?'

Duryodhana ground his teeth in rage. 'Did you see the way those stupid kings were fawning over Yudhishthira? And what arrogance he exuded as he sat on his throne, as if he were not a mere mortal, but Lord Indra himself. Uncle, my life does not seem worth living any more. I will not be at peace till I wage war on these upstarts and grind them into the dust!' he cried, slamming a fist on the arm of his chair.

'Calm down, dear nephew. War is an uncertain business. I have a better plan,' Shakuni replied. A smug smile spread over his face as he continued, 'A plan that will completely destroy the Pandavas without any bloodshed or loss of life. You do know that Yudhishthira has a weakness for the game of dice, even though he's quite useless at it.'

'And you are the best in the land!' Duryodhana exclaimed exultantly. 'What a brilliant idea. I will send an invitation immediately.'

However, he needed to consult his father about this. Dhritirashtra was reluctant at first, but finally agreed. Vidura was asked to carry the invitation. He had strong reservations about the plan and told his older brother frankly that he feared it would lead to needless strife among the cousins. Dhritirashtra replied smoothly that destiny ruled all, so he should not question this decision.

Full of misgivings, Vidura arrived at Indraprastha. Yudhishthira rose at once to greet him respectfully. 'Is all well in Hastinapur? Why is your face dark with gloom, dear uncle?' he asked.

Vidura sighed. 'As well as it can be, Yudhishthira, for the time being,' he said, his voice sombre. 'I wish I had not been asked to convey this invitation. Duryodhana has proposed a game of dice and your uncle commanded me to bid you to participate. He has erected a beautiful hall at Jayantapura and has requested you to come and see it and enjoy a game of dice with your brothers. I fear that there is no kindly sentiment behind this request. Games of chance only lead to quarrels and ruin. Please heed my warning before accepting this invitation,' he cautioned.

The Pandavas exchanged glances. They knew that there could not be any goodwill behind an invitation from Duryodhana. But there was little choice in the matter. Besides, Yudhishthira was inflicted with a weakness for gambling, so the temptation was great.

'You are right to warn us, uncle,' he said thoughtfully. 'However, it will not be polite if I refuse this seemingly friendly request. My uncle and cousins might take offence and that itself could lead to a quarrel. The wise Vyasa himself warned me not to create any situation that would lead to strife with my cousins. And then, you are aware of the kshatriya code of conduct. If I refuse a challenge, it will be taken as cowardice.'

So, despite being cautioned by the well-meaning Vidura, Yudhishthira and his brothers set off for Hastinapur. They received an outwardly warm welcome and were accommodated in a luxurious palace. The game was fixed for the next day.

Yudhishthira and his brothers arrived at the appointed time at the hall that had been newly built at Jayantapura, which lay on the outskirts of Hastinapur. They admired it with due courtesy but it was obvious that their cousins were keen to start the game of dice, rather than spend time on polite conversation.

'Come, Yudhishthira, now it is time for some pleasurable activities,' Duryodhana began. 'I know you love a game of dice. So, shall we while away some time on this sport?'

'Dear cousin,' Yudhishthira replied tactfully, 'you know that a wise man does not waste time on a game of chance. Gambling is a vice, and can become an addiction, like wine. Such pastimes have unpleasant consequences and lead to arguments and quarrels. I would prefer not to play.'

Shakuni laughed mockingly when he heard this. 'The mighty Yudhishthira has just performed the Rajasuya yagna. His treasury is bursting with gold and jewels. It seems he is afraid that if he lays a wager, he might lose all his newly acquired wealth. It's all right. We will understand if you are afraid to accept our challenge.'

The words twisted in Yudhishthira's heart like a sharp dagger. 'Who says I am afraid? I was only reminding you of the evils that result from such sports. After all, in the end it is a man's fate that determines the outcome. I accept your challenge.'

Duryodhana and Shakuni exchanged triumphant smiles. 'Come then,' Duryodhana said quickly. 'What are we waiting for?'

A dazzling white cloth had been spread in the middle of the hall. It was surrounded by thick carpets for the spectators to sit upon, and silk bolsters for them to recline against. Attendants stood around, waiting to offer the guests refreshing drinks and the choicest delicacies.

The air was taut with expectation. Everyone loved the thrill of a game of chance.

Yudhishthira had earlier asked Vidura whom he might have to face. 'Who will play with me? You, Duryodhana?' he now inquired.

His cousin replied, 'I will provide the stakes in the form of cash and jewels. It is my uncle Shakuni who will play on my behalf.'

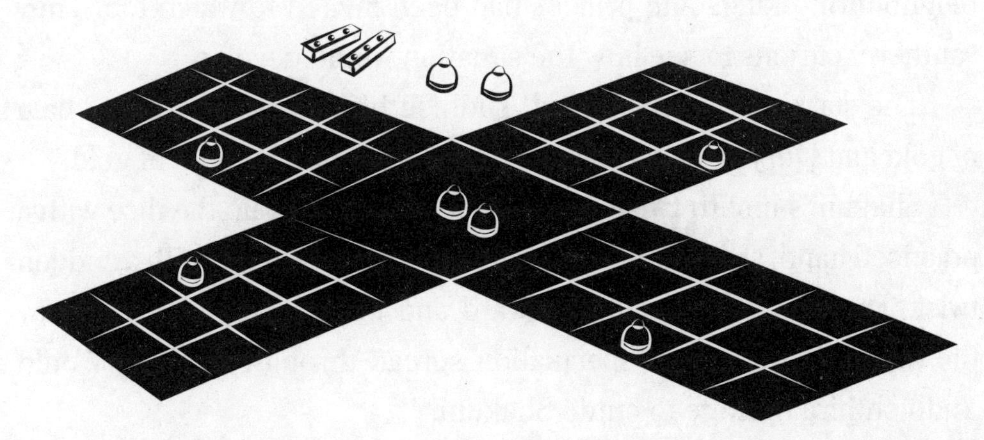

The Pandavas froze in their seats. Everyone knew that Shakuni was the most accomplished player in the land. It was even rumoured that his dice had magical qualities.

Yudhishthira was trapped. He would have had some chance of defeating Duryodhana; however, against Shakuni he saw little hope. He made a last try. 'Duryodhana, you sent the invitation. I came here expecting to face you in the game. It is not an acceptable practice for one player to substitute for another.'

Shakuni sniggered scornfully. 'You seem to be searching for new excuses not to play,' he said.

The insult stung Yudhishthira. 'I am not making excuses. Did I say I won't play?' With a heavy heart, he assumed a seat opposite Shakuni and his cousin.

The elders of the family—Dhritirashtra, Bhishma and Vidura as well as the gurus Drona and Kripa—were all present. They knew this game would have an ugly end but felt powerless to prevent it. Many neighbouring kings and princes had been invited to watch too. They sat there, curious to see how the situation would develop.

The stakes were announced. Yudhishthira pledged a heavy chain of gold and Duryodhana replied, 'I wager a similar amount of gold.'

Shakuni's mouth twisted in a smile as he swept up the dice with a practiced hand, shook them and rolled them on the cloth with a sudden twist. The spectators leaned forward and exclaimed when they saw the numbers. A buzz of speculation spread through the hall. Would Yudhishthira manage to outdo Shakuni?

Yudhishthira reached out, rather hesitantly. As the dice fell, somewhat clumsily, the Pandavas suppressed a groan. 'I win!' Shakuni cried exultantly.

'What will you bet next?' Duryodhana asked, as Yudhishthira removed the chain from around his neck and handed it to his cousin.

'This flawless diamond ring,' Yudhishthira replied grimly.

Shakuni nodded and said, 'Here you go!'

The dice rolled from his fingers in a swift graceful movement. It was another unbeatable throw. But Yudhishthira had no choice but to try his luck again. And once again, he lost.

'What is your next wager?' Duryodhana asked as he grabbed the precious ring and slipped it on to his finger.

'This bag of gold coins,' Yudhishthira said, nonchalantly.

'Good enough,' Duryodhana shrugged. 'Come on, uncle. What are you waiting for?'

Shakuni scooped the dice between his cupped hands and shook them till they rattled. Then he flung them on the cloth. There was a gasp of astonishment from the audience.

'Try and beat this, cousin!' Duryodhana smirked.

Yudhishthira's hands shook as he picked up the dice. He was praying fervently, but a sinking feeling was taking hold of him. How could he hope to defeat an expert like Shakuni? The man was truly a magician with the dice. People alleged that he whispered a mantra over them, others said they were made of his father Subal's bones so his spirit moved them, but this had never been proved.

The dice almost fell out of Yudhishthira's hand and the numbers that revealed themselves made his heart plummet to the depths. He felt as if he was trapped in a quagmire which was sucking him in deeper and deeper.

'I win again!' Shakuni's cry of victory did not evoke any applause from the spectators. There was only a strained silence as the guests exchanged apprehensive glances.

Yudhishthira and Shakuni continued to play and the atmosphere became more and more tense as Shakuni won game after game. And with each game, Yudhishthira became poorer and poorer. He lost all the gold and jewels he staked, then his horses and his elephants, then his chariots, weapons and even his army. In fact, the time came when he was stripped of everything he owned.

Then the right-thinking Vidura stood up and addressed Dhritirashtra. 'Your majesty, don't you think it's time to stop this unequal and unjust game? This greed will have terrible consequences for the family and the country. I beg you, ask your son and his uncle to put an end to this.'

Dhritirashtra made no reply to this and an electric silence fell over the whole assembly. But Duryodhana addressed Vidura in insolent tones: 'Dear uncle, I know how partial you are to my cousins. You have always been against me and now you are poisoning my father's mind. Kindly leave us alone and let destiny take its course.'

Shakuni sniggered and said: 'The great king Yudhishthira who lately performed the Rajasuya yagna is no better than a pauper now. Am I wrong, Yudhishthira, or do you have anything left to stake?'

The words cut Yudhishthira to the core. A desperate impulse took hold of him, an impulse typical of one in the grip of a game of chance. Maybe I can make up my losses, he thought, maybe my luck will change.

'Yes, I do!' he said sharply and everyone sat up. 'I wager my handsome young brother, Nakula.'

This was such a shameful wager that the assembled princes stared at each other in disbelief. 'Has he lost his mind, the wise and righteous Yudhishthira?' they whispered.

As anticipated, Nakula was lost and Shakuni and Duryodhana's laughter rang through the hall. The madness had taken such a strong hold of Yudhishthira that he did not stop at Nakula. One by one, Sahadeva, Arjuna, and Bhima were offered up and lost to Duryodhana. Finally, in a last gamble, Yudhishthira staked himself.

And he lost again. 'I have nothing more to offer,' he said, faint with despair.

Shakuni narrowed his gaze as he looked at the helpless king. 'There is someone else,' he said slowly, 'your wife Draupadi. You can put her at stake.'

Bhima gripped his mace and made as if to hurl it at Shakuni, but Arjuna threw a warning glance at him.

Utterly desperate, Yudhishthira was unable to think straight. Maybe Draupadi would be the auspicious wager that would change his fortune. 'All right,' he replied in an almost inaudible voice.

Once again, the dice was rolled and Yudhishthira's luck did not turn. As he stared disbelievingly at what he had thrown, Shakuni shouted with joy. 'I have won Draupadi!' he bellowed.

An ominous silence descended on the hall. It was soon drowned out by the triumphant cries of the Kauravas. Bhishma and Vidura sat there stunned. The right-thinking guests among those gathered there exchanged horrified glances at this ghastly outcome.

Duryodhana could not stop smiling as he embraced Shakuni. 'Uncle,' he exclaimed, 'this is the happiest day of my life! You are the one who made this possible.'

He turned to Vidura and said arrogantly: 'Now it's your turn to do something for me. Go and fetch my slave Draupadi from the women's chambers.'

Vidura shook his head in disgust. 'There is still time to end this madness, Duryodhana. Your actions are an open invitation to disaster. Do not play with fire.'

'This lowborn man can only whine,' Duryodhana said mockingly. He summoned an attendant and said, 'Go and tell Draupadi that she belongs to me now. She must appear before us without delay.'

The servant headed to the women's chambers and asked for Draupadi. 'Kindly come with me,' he said, 'you are Duryodhana's slave now.'

Draupadi was dumbfounded. 'What is this nonsense I am hearing?' she cried, when she recovered from the shock. 'How can I, the wife of the Pandavas, be considered Duryodhana's slave?'

'Your husband Yudhishthira has lost all he owned in the game of dice,' replied the servant. 'When nothing was left, he wagered his brothers, then himself and finally, he lost you too. You belong to the Kaurava prince now.'

Draupadi shrieked with rage. 'How can this be possible?'

'It happened in front of me, Draupadi,' the servant said.

'If that is true, kindly go and ask my husband whether he wagered himself first or me. I will not move from here till I have my answer,' Draupadi said firmly.

The attendant returned to court. 'Draupadi has a question for Yudhishthira,' he said. 'She wants to know if Yudhishthira lost himself before he put her at stake.'

Yudhishthira felt as if he would die of shame. What had he done? Crazed by the desire to make good his losses, he had sunk deeper and deeper into the pit and compromised the future of those he held most dear. He did not know what reply to make. Technically, Draupadi was right. If he had already lost himself, he had no right to wager his wife.

Duryodhana flew into a rage. 'Tell that woman to come and ask the question herself,' he yelled.

The attendant was already sickened by the course of events, but did not dare oppose his employer. He reluctantly made his way to the women's chambers. 'Gracious Draupadi,' he said, 'I fear that our prince is inviting his own destruction. He says you should come and ask your husband himself.'

'I will not come,' Draupadi said, 'unless my husband summons me. Kindly ask him what I am to do.'

The man returned and put the question to Yudhishthira. The oldest Pandava hung his head in shame. 'Tell her to come and ask the elders of the court whether I acted correctly when I put her at stake after losing myself,' he said in a low voice.

Duryodhana was running out of patience, however. He turned to his brother Dussashana. 'Go and drag that conceited woman here, if she refuses to come,' he said furiously. 'She is our slave and must obey our orders.'

Dussashana rushed out of the hall and barged into Draupadi's chambers. 'Why are you acting so coy, lady?' he said with a mocking laugh. 'You belong to my brother now. Come with me.'

Draupadi sprang up and ran towards Gandhari's chambers to appeal to the lady for justice. But Dussashana grabbed her by her hair. 'Can't you take a straight order? I told you, you are our slave now!' he barked.

'Leave me alone, Dussashana!' Draupadi screamed. 'Don't touch me. My hair has been purified by the waters of the Rajasuya. It is sacrilege to touch it.'

'All that is meaningless now,' Dussashana snarled.

Mercilessly, he pulled the shrieking and protesting Draupadi into the assembly hall.

As she was forced to enter the hall in this piteous state, Draupadi looked around and took note of all the grandees collected there. Even as Dussashana grinned with triumph and flung an insolent glance at his elders, Draupadi managed to catch her breath and control her weeping.

'Bhishma Pitamah, uncle Dhritirashtra, venerable gurus Kripa and Drona, you have sat through the vile game of dice that was played here. How did you allow my husband to stake me in this shameful manner? It was bad enough that he was trapped into playing and cheated by these wicked men. But if he had already surrendered his freedom, how could he place a wager on his wife? Answer me, wise elders!' Her large eyes flashed with rage as she said this. 'Answer, and if you ever loved and respected your mothers or wives, sisters or daughters, do not abandon me to these sinful creatures.'

A sob tore out of her throat and while the elders hung their heads in shame, Bhima let out a roar. He could not control himself any longer. He turned to Yudhishthira and cried, 'Even the most lowdown gambler would not stake a woman in a game. And you, a supposedly righteous king, have thrown the daughter of Drupada to these dogs! Bring me fire, Sahadeva, I want to burn the accursed hands that cast the dice.'

Arjuna immediately interposed. 'Dear Bhima,' he said softly. 'Control yourself. You know our brother never indulges in wrong actions. He has been snared in the trap set by Duryodhana and Shakuni. We must remain united in the face of our enemies.'

Somehow Bhima calmed himself. Just then, Vikarna, one of the Kauravas, stood up to speak. 'O brave kshatriyas, why are you silent?' he said. 'I know I am one of the youngest amongst you but I can clearly see what an evil plan has unfolded before us. Duryodhana's invitation was a plot and the game a ruse to ruin the Pandavas. The truth is, Draupadi is not Yudhishthira's wife alone. Also, he had already become Duryodhana's slave, so owned no possessions to stake. And, it was Shakuni who suggested the wager, which is against the rules of the game.'

His words evoked a burst of applause from the assembly. 'Well spoken! Dharma has been saved by these words!' many cried out.

However, Karna, motivated by his hatred of the Pandavas, immediately contradicted Vikarna.

This hatred went a long way back. As a student of Drona, Karna had once entered an archery competition against Arjuna. However, when he was asked to proclaim his lineage, he was at a loss. Karna had been brought up by Radha, a charioteer, and thus could not compete with the blue-blooded Arjuna. To win him over, Duryodhana had immediately proclaimed him king of Anga. But when Karna was being crowned, Bhima mocked his father, the charioteer. Ever since, Karna had detested the Pandavas, while being unwaveringly loyal to Duryodhana. Little did the Pandavas know that Karna was actually their brother – Kunti's son from Surya, the Sun god.

'How dare you speak thus in the presence of your elders?' Karna snarled. 'You do not know what you are talking about, disloyal youth. You are turning against your own brothers. If Yudhishthira had lost himself, he had lost all he owned including his wife. Draupadi and all his possessions, including the clothes on her body, belong to Shakuni now. Dussashana, remove all their clothes and give them to Shakuni.'

At these cruel words, the Pandavas flung off their clothes to show they had fulfilled the conditions of the wager.

Dussashana then leapt at Draupadi, full of malicious glee. He began to pull at her garments, even while the whole assembly gasped in outrage. Draupadi looked around helplessly. When no one came to her aid she wailed: 'O Lord of the world, protector of the weak, save my honour!' Then she fainted.

Dussashana shamelessly continued to try and strip her, as all the men covered their eyes in horror. But even as he tugged at her sari, it seemed to grow longer and longer and no matter how hard he pulled, Draupadi remained fully clad. Dussashana sweated with the effort, his arms ached and a huge pile of cloth accumulated, dwarfing him.

Cries of 'A miracle!' 'A miracle! Praise be to the Lord of the World!' erupted around the hall.

Finally, shaken and utterly exhausted, Dussashana collapsed on to the floor. At that moment, Bhima swore a terrible vow: 'May I never be reunited with my ancestors till I drink the blood of this sinful man.'

Then the fully clad Draupadi rose from the ground and even as she thanked Lord Krishna, her saviour, she added her own oath. 'I swear never to bind my hair till I bathe it in Dussashana's blood.'

Even as Bhima and Draupadi made these vows, the cries of jackals and donkeys rang through the hall.

On hearing these ill-omened sounds, a shuddering Dhritirashtra now tried to make peace. He told Yudhishthira and his brothers that they should return to their capital Indraprastha, with all their possessions intact.

The Pandavas left, but Duryodhana raged at his father for ruining his plan. He forced the king to agree to send another invitation to Yudhishthira to play a game of dice.

The five brothers had barely reached their kingdom, when the sound of a horse's hooves resounded in their ears. It was a messenger sent by Dhritirashtra.

'Your majesty,' he addressed Yudhishthira, bowing low. 'I have an invitation from your illustrious uncle. He has requested that you come and play another game of dice.'

The brothers, who were still numb after their terrible ordeal, stared at each other in disbelief.

'It seems that our fate has something in store that we cannot avoid,' Yudhishthira said with a sigh, trying to be stoic. 'Whatever it is, good or evil, we have to face it.' His brothers remained silent, though bitter thoughts raced through their minds. 'Tell the king we accept,' Yudhishthira finally said to the messenger, his voice grim.

Once again, the Pandavas made their way to Hastinapur, their hearts heavier than on the previous visit.

Once again, Duryodhana and Shakuni welcomed them with evil grins. 'I knew you would not refuse, cousin,' Duryodhana said. 'You would not go against the dharma of a kshatriya.'

Bhima muttered something unintelligible under his breath, even as Arjuna threw him a warning glance.

'Ready to try your luck again, Yudhishthira?' Shakuni smirked, idly jingling the dice in his hand. 'We have made the stakes easier this time. If you lose, you have to go into exile in the forest for twelve years and spend the thirteenth year in disguise. If you are identified in this final year, you will forfeit your kingdom. Is that right, Duryodhana?'

Duryodhana nodded. 'Absolutely. Is this acceptable, O Yudhishthira?'

What could Yudhishthira say but 'yes'?

Once again, the fateful dice were rolled. Once again, Yudhishthira played and lost. And once again, the unfortunate Pandavas had to pay the price and were compelled to go into exile.

The Vessel of Plenty

After the fateful game of dice, the exiled Pandavas had walked away from Hastinapur, trying to keep a brave face. Once again, the people of Hastinapur lamented the departure of their beloved princes. It was not easy for the five brothers and Draupadi to accept the injustice behind this forced exile, but they had little choice in the matter. Accompanied by brahmins, they reached a small copse called Pramanavata that lay on the banks of the Ganga and rested in the shade of the trees. There was nothing for them to eat, only the water of the holy river to quench their thirst.

Several brahmins had insisted on coming along with them to the forest. They too had to remain without any food. This situation was very painful for Yudhishthira. The next morning, he pleaded with the brahmins to return to the city. 'I beg you to leave us to our fate,' he said with folded hands. 'You know we have been banished for twelve years. I have no means to feed you as I used to. We ourselves will have to forage for berries and roots in the forest to sustain ourselves. Please don't add the sin of inhospitality to our woes.'

The brahmins, however, refused to leave them. 'O gracious Yudhishthira, please don't ask us to abandon you. We want to suffer this banishment along with you.'

Deeply disturbed, Yudhishthira consulted his guru Dhaumya. 'Why don't you pray to the Sun god, Yudhishthira?' Dhaumya advised. 'It is the Sun that provides us with food through its life-giving light. If you appeal to the Sun god for help, he is sure to pay heed to your entreaty.'

Yudhishthira then embarked on a fervent prayer to the Sun god. He prayed day and night without eating or sleeping. At last, the god was moved by his devotion and appeared before him in a vision.

'Yudhishthira, your dedication to the welfare of those around you has pleased me greatly,' he said. 'I will provide you with food for the twelve years of your exile. Take this copper vessel – the Akshay Patra. Once a day, it will fill up with food for as many people as you wish to feed. From the moment Draupadi begins to serve you and your guests, till she herself has eaten, the vessel will provide an abundant supply of nourishment.'

From that day, Yudhishthira was able to feed all the people who accompanied him. Many years passed by and thanks to the Sun god's boon, they never lacked sustenance.

After he had tricked the Pandavas into exile, Duryodhana began to feel that he was the supreme ruler of the land. Drunk with power, he wanted to perform the Rajasuya yagna. However, he was advised by his gurus that he could not do this while his father and Yudhishthira were alive, so he had to content himself with the lesser Vaishnava yagna.

Sometime after the completion of this ceremony, the sage Durvasa decided to visit Duryodhana along with ten thousand of his disciples. He was well known for his irascible nature. Durvasa had the tendency to fly into a rage on the slightest pretext and curse the unfortunate person who had fallen foul of him. In fact, he would deliberately make things uncomfortable for his hosts so he could find a chance to complain. Knowing this, Duryodhana took extra care to entertain the sage and his disciples as lavishly as he could. Considering the means he had at his disposal as ruler of Hastinapur, this was not a difficult task for him. However, he did not want to take any chances and attended to Durvasa personally, making sure that every whim was fulfilled. The result was that the bad-tempered sage was extremely pleased with Duryodhana. When it was time for him to leave—after the most sumptuous food and the choicest of entertainment—Durvasa showered praise and blessings upon his host.

Even though he had nothing to fear from his cousins during their period of exile, the malicious Duryodhana was always on the lookout for ways to stir up trouble for the Pandavas. It struck him that if he suggested that the cantankerous sage visit Yudhishthira, his impoverished cousin would be caught unprepared. Duryodhana was confident that the Pandavas would not be able to match up to the hospitality Durvasa received at Hastinapur and this would provoke him to hand out a curse that would add to the brothers' woes.

So, just as the sage was about to depart with his retinue, Duryodhana said, after bowing low at Durvasa's feet, 'Venerable sir, I thank you for favouring us with your gracious presence and granting us your blessings. My cousins, the Pandavas, are living in the forest these days. Please grant them the boon of a visit as well so they too might receive the benefit of your good wishes.'

Duryodhana had, of course, heard about the vessel of plenty. But he also knew that it could only be used once a day. Cunningly, he recommended that the sage visit at a time when he was sure that the Pandavas would have eaten and the vessel would be empty.

'That was a master stroke,' Karna observed, as Durvasa departed with his huge entourage in tow. 'How I would love to be there, to gloat over the curses the sage is bound to favour them with!'

'Blessings for us and curses for our enemies!' Shakuni shrieked with laughter. 'I too am tempted to follow this army to see the fun.'

'Ha, ha!' Duryodhana joined his uncle in mocking his cousins. 'Let's see how those beggars entertain Durvasa and his ten thousand men in the middle of the forest. I can imagine them rushing to dig up roots for the sage to chew upon and experiencing the fiery blast of his anger.'

It was late afternoon by the time Durvasa found the Pandavas in the forest. They had long finished their lunch. Draupadi first served the brahmins and any guests that might be visiting, and then the brothers. She was the last to eat. After that, she scoured the Akshay Patra clean and put it away.

The whole family was resting when the sound of Durvasa's entourage on the march made them sit up with a start.

Yudhishthira hurried out with his brothers following close behind. When Durvasa's massive frame became visible from behind the trees and the chattering voices of his disciples were heard, the Pandavas exchanged apprehensive glances.

'From where has this calamity descended upon us?' Bhima muttered.

'Hush, Bhima, he might hear what you're saying,' Yudhishthira said anxiously. 'We will have to face it somehow.' His words sounded brave but his face had turned ashen.

Durvasa was at their doorstep now, and the brothers hurried to prostrate themselves at his feet, before greeting the horde of disciples, all of whom were gazing at them curiously.

'Welcome, venerable sir, to our humble abode!' Yudhishthira had to force the words out. 'It is a hot day. Please come and rest for a while. Do let us know how we can make you comfortable.'

'It was a long walk from Hastinapur,' Durvasa replied, stroking his beard. 'We are all completely famished. But first, we would like to go and have a wash in the river. In the meantime, you can prepare a meal for us.'

Stupefied, the Pandavas watched the host depart.

'He had to choose this time to come,' Bhima growled. 'When the Akshay Patra is empty for the day. If only the Sun god had allowed it to brim over any time of the day, whenever we needed food!'

'I think the timing is deliberate,' Arjuna said furiously. 'They are coming from Hastinapur. No doubt our beloved Duryodhana pointed their steps this way.'

'Whatever made them visit us,' Yudhishthira said with his usual patience, 'they are our guests. They are hungry. We have to provide food for them. Draupadi, is there anything left?'

Draupadi had overheard the entire conversation and came rushing out. 'Nothing,' she said dejectedly, shaking her head. 'I finished eating five minutes ago and have just cleaned the pot. Why couldn't they have come a little earlier? As if we didn't have enough problems to cope with. Now this ill-tempered man will curse us and make us even more miserable!' She slumped to the ground in despair. 'O Krishna,' she wailed, 'won't you save us from Durvasa's fury?'

The words were barely out of Draupadi's mouth when Krishna appeared, smiling as usual. 'Hurry, Draupadi,' he said, before she could speak, 'I'm starving! Bring me some food right away.'

Draupadi struck her forehead with her palm. 'Is there no end to our sorrows?' she wept. 'I asked you for help and now you are adding to our problems. There is no food, Krishna. The vessel the Sun god gifted us has exhausted its supply for the day. And as soon as I had washed it, this awful Durvasa appeared along with ten thousand

disciples. Shall I feed that army with air? That's all I can offer. And now, you come too, saying you are hungry.'

'I am absolutely ravenous, Draupadi,' Krishna said. 'Now stop making excuses and bring me the Akshay Patra, so I can see for myself if it is actually empty.'

'You don't believe me? All right, see for yourself!' Draupadi rose and fetched the vessel.

Krishna examined it carefully. 'How can the Akshay Patra go empty?' he said with a twinkle in his eye. He pointed to the grain of rice and piece of vegetable sticking to the bottom of the pot. Then he picked up the tiny morsel of food and put it in his mouth.

Draupadi flushed with embarrassment at the thought that she had been careless about scouring the pot thoroughly. Then her mouth dropped open as she watched Krishna rubbing his belly as if he had consumed a large meal. 'There, my hunger is satiated,' he said. 'My heartfelt thanks for this delicious meal, dear Draupadi.'

Meanwhile, the Pandavas had been pacing up and down outside, tense with the thought that Durvasa might return any moment now, and rain curses on them for their lack of hospitality.

Bhima's ears pricked up when he heard Krishna calling out to him. 'Bhima, go and call the sage and his followers. Tell them that their meal is ready and will be served the moment they arrive.'

Bhima gaped at Krishna. But he well knew that Krishna always provided a solution, even in the worst of times, so he didn't ask anything and instead hurried to the river.

There he found the sage and his enormous band of disciples splashing about contentedly in the water.

'Venerable sir,' he said, 'I have come to invite you and your disciples for your meal. The food is ready.'

'Our meal?' To Bhima's utter astonishment, the irritable Durvasa actually smiled. 'Thank you very much, Bhima, but I find that I'm not at all hungry now.'

His disciples too surrounded them saying, 'We feel as replete as if we had feasted on the most delicious dishes in the world. There is no space left in our bellies. And we're enjoying bathing in the Ganga so much.'

Durvasa raised his hand in blessing. 'Please convey my apologies to the noble Yudhishthira. I'm sorry I caused him trouble. But I too feel as full as if I have partaken of a sumptuous meal.'

The sage realised that a miracle had occurred, which could only be the result of divine intervention. He was ashamed now that he had tried to test the destitute Pandavas at Duryodhana's suggestion.

When Krishna, in whom the whole universe was contained, satisfied his hunger with a grain of rice and a tiny shred of vegetable, all beings felt that their hunger had been sated too.

Thus, once again, Krishna had come to the aid of the harried Pandavas.

The Divine Weapons

Krishna's timely appearance during Durvasa's visit was not the first time he had met the Pandavas in the forest. In fact, shortly after the Pandavas had built a hermitage for themselves in the forest, he had arrived at their dwelling to commiserate with them. While the fateful game of dice was playing itself out, he had been entangled in a battle with Salva who had besieged Dwarka. Thus, he had not been able to come to their aid earlier. Deeply saddened by their fate, Krishna wiped Draupadi's tears and promised the Pandavas that the Kauravas would face terrible destruction for their vile actions. Draupadi was somewhat consoled but it was still hard for the family to reconcile themselves to their fate.

Yudhishthira suggested that they retire deep into the woods, far from human habitation, where only the sages lived. Thus, they took up residence in the forest of Dwaitavana – a place that resounded with the chanting of the Vedas and sacred hymns. It was here that Yudhishthira managed to find some peace. However, this was not the case with the others. Bhima, Arjuna and Draupadi often argued with Yudhishthira when he told them to surrender to their destiny and accept what it had ordained for them.

'It is the duty of a kshatriya to fight with his enemies,' Bhima raged. 'And here we sit, like helpless puppets, allowing those dastardly Kauravas to revel in our misfortune. A promise extracted through deceitful means should not be honoured.'

'Bhima is right,' Arjuna would reply. 'Those vile creatures have grabbed our kingdom using unfair means. How can we give up and not fight for what is ours? The dishonour we have all suffered should be immediately avenged. The thought that we sit here passively, doing nothing to gain redress for the horrors perpetrated on all of us, scorches me day and night. We have forgotten what the dharma of kshatriyas is. Why shouldn't we pay them back for the shameful treatment meted out to Draupadi?'

Draupadi too would rave and rant and shed bitter tears. 'I cannot bear to see you living like a mendicant,' she would tell Yudhishthira. 'You who were the mightiest king in Bharatavarsha. And look at Bhima, the strongest of men, wasting away without proper food to eat! An accomplished warrior like Arjuna has nothing better to do than throw pebbles into a pond. And skilled swordsmen like Nakula and Sahadeva spend their time gathering wild fruit. Is this the life we all deserve?'

However, Yudhishthira would reply patiently, 'Draupadi, do you think my heart is not ravaged with pain thinking about the suffering my actions have brought upon all of you? But I made a promise – that we would spend twelve years in the forest and one year in disguise. I cannot go back on my word.'

'So much for this dharma of yours!' Bhima lashed out. 'Those who indulged in false and evil deeds are enjoying our kingdom. Don't you understand that by cheating you, they have forfeited any claim to righteous conduct on our part? We can spend twelve years here somehow. But how will we hide our identity for a year? Just think of Draupadi's plight, a princess who has no other choice but to cover herself with tree bark. I beg of you, brother, let us take up our weapons and regain our kingdom.'

Yudhishthira fell silent for a while. Then he said, 'It is entirely my fault, Bhima, that all of you have to suffer in this manner. But all your arguments will not convince me to swerve from my promise.'

These words flung Draupadi, Bhima and Arjuna into a deeper state of despair. As they sat there disconsolately, they noticed the venerable sage Vyasa approaching.

They rose immediately and greeted him by prostrating themselves at his feet. Vyasa raised his hands to bless them. 'I know how difficult it is for you to put up with this injustice,' he said. 'You long for vengeance.

However, this is not the right time to wage war on the Kauravas. They have many powerful allies. Remember, too, that Bhishma and Drona will fight on their side, as well as Karna and Ashwatthama – all highly-trained warriors. You have to make extensive preparations for this war in order to win it.'

These soothing words brought a spark of hope to Bhima's eyes and Arjuna perked up too. What Vyasa suggested next cheered up the brothers even more.'Arjuna, it is time for you to embark on a penance to please Lord Shiva and receive the blessing of the invincible Pasupata weapon,' Vyasa said. 'Your father Indra will grant you many weapons too, and make you invincible in battle. I advise you to return to the Kamyaka forest now.'

The Pandavas took Vyasa's advice. They returned to Kamyaka, from where Arjuna took leave of his brothers and set off for the mountains in the north. When he reached a peak named Indrakila, he felt it was a good place to conduct his penance. While he was looking around for a suitable spot, he came upon an ascetic.

'Why have you come here, young warrior?' the man asked. 'This peaceful mountain is meant to be the abode of men who have renounced the world. But you are clad in armour and are carrying bows and arrows. This is a place where people attempt to subdue their passions, not make war on others. Kindly discard your weapons.'

Arjuna bowed respectfully to the old brahmin. 'Venerable sage, I have come here to seek weapons that I can use in a righteous war,' he said.

At this, the ascetic revealed himself to be Indra, Arjuna's father. 'What is the use of seeking weapons, my son?' he said, blessing him. 'Come with me and enjoy all the pleasures of Indralok.'

'O great king of the gods, I thank you, but divine pleasures are meaningless for me,' Arjuna said respectfully. 'I have left my wife Draupadi and my brothers in the forest, suffering the greatest privation. I want arms that will help me to regain our kingdom, unfairly snatched away by our cousins, the Kauravas.'

'My son, you must travel further and embark on a sincere penance to gain Lord Shiva's favour. He will grant you the most invincible weapon.' Saying this, thousand-eyed Indra departed.

Arjuna now headed towards the high Himalayas. When he found a suitable spot, he assumed the lotus posture and began to pray to Shiva.

He had been praying for a long time when a wild boar suddenly attacked him. This was actually a rakshasa who had adopted this form. Furious that his penance had been disrupted, Arjuna picked up his Gandiva bow and shot an arrow at the boar. Just then a wild-looking hunter appeared on the scene, with a woman by his side.

The hunter, too, let loose an arrow at the same time, which also pierced the boar. When the two arrows entered the body of the boar simultaneously, it was as if two streaks of lightning had flashed down the mountain side.

'Who are you?' Arjuna cried, outraged. 'How dare you shoot at the boar that I was targeting?'

'I have been chasing this boar for some time,' said the hunter, 'and it is my rightful prey. Who are *you*? You do not look like a forest dweller. Your body looks soft and pampered.'

'You may say what you like, but it was my arrow that killed the boar,' Arjuna insisted.

The hunter simply laughed. 'It was my arrow that hit the target first,' he said. 'The boar belongs to me and so does your arrow. You will have to defeat me to prove your point.'

By now Arjuna was spoiling for a fight. He rose and let loose a cloud of arrows that covered the hunter completely, like writhing snakes. To his astonishment, the hunter simply brushed them away. Still, Arjuna was not prepared to give up so easily. He went on shooting till all his arrows were spent. Furious to find his quiver completely empty, he hurled his bow at the hunter, but it bounced off the man's head without hurting him. Arjuna then swung his sword at his adversary, but it glanced off without leaving a single scratch.

Arjuna was becoming more and more enraged. He tore branches off trees to rain blows at the hunter, picked up rocks and flung them at his opponent. But none of these injured the man, who just stood there with an infuriating smile on his face.

Finally, Arjuna challenged him to a wrestling bout. But to his dismay, the hunter's body was as hard as iron. Arjuna could not grapple with him and was soon felled to the ground. As he lay there, gasping, covered with blood and too weak to even get up, he sent a silent prayer to Lord Shiva to save him from this terrible foe.

And then, all of a sudden, the truth dawned upon him. The hunter was none other than Shiva himself! Arjuna rose with an effort and fell at his feet. He begged for forgiveness for battling the god.

Shiva raised him up and blessed him. Then he returned his Gandiva bow to him. 'My son, you have more than proved your mettle,' he said. 'Ask for any boon that you desire.'

'Lord, I pray you to grant me a vision of your real form,' Arjuna said.

Shiva then assumed his godly shape, with Parvati by his side. He placed his hands on Arjuna, healing all his wounds and making him stronger than ever with his touch. He also granted him the boon of the invincible Pasupata weapon and taught him all the mantras for sending it forth and bringing it back.

'Now go and pay your respects to your father,' he said. 'He is expecting you.'

Even as Shiva was speaking, a luminous glow began to envelop the mountain. To Arjuna's astonishment and delight, it was the gods who were descending to bless him. Varuna, Yama, Kubera and his own father Indra. All of them granted him the use of their special weapons. Then Indra's charioteer Matali arrived to transport him to his father's kingdom. When he reached Amravati, Arjuna was awestruck by its grandeur. He was ushered into his father's court and drank in all its wonders wide-eyed. As he watched the Apsaras perform their divine dances, life in the forest seemed remote and distant. Then an extraordinary thing happened. When the Apsara Urvashi set eyes on him, she instantly fell in love with the young warrior.

Urvashi did not lose much time in sharing her feelings. Arjuna was taken aback at first. Then he replied courteously, 'Respected lady, I can only think of you as a mother, because you were the beloved of my ancestor Pururavas.'

Furious at the rejection, Urvashi cursed him. 'You have dared to reject me!' she cried. 'For this, I curse you to turn into a eunuch, and spend your time amongst women, dancing and singing.'

Arjuna was stunned. A warrior like him to become a eunuch! Utterly dejected, he decided to seek out his friend, Gandharva Chitrasena, and share his predicament with him. 'You have been able to resist Urvashi,' Chitrasena said with a smile. 'It is a great achievement. Even the most venerable sages were not immune to her charms. And as for the curse, do not worry. When her anger cools down, I will ask her to reduce it to one year. It will come in useful when you need to hide your identity during the last year of your exile.'

Chitrasena taught Arjuna many of the fine arts like singing and dancing and trained him to play various musical instruments. Arjuna also performed many tasks for his father like subduing the Nivatakavachas Asuras, who were troubling Indra. Arjuna travelled down to their city under the ocean and used the Mohini weapon to outwit their magic. Indra had also taught him the use of many other divine weapons, including his vajra or thunderbolt, with which Arjuna finally destroyed the Asuras.

Arjuna spent a long time with Indra in Amravati. The Pandavas and Draupadi missed him a great deal. However, they knew that this stay with his father was crucial for all of them. They badly needed the help of the divine weapons to prevail in the eventual war with the Kauravas.

In the meantime, Yudhishthira was advised by Narada and the sage Lomasa to go on a pilgrimage. The family set off, visiting all the holy places. Bhima performed many feats of valour during this time. Finally, they reached the Mandara mountain.

It was here that they had a joyful reunion with Arjuna. He had a lot to share with them about his eventful stay with his father.

Ten years had passed by now and only two more years of exile were left. The Pandavas decided to leave Badri ashram, where they had been staying, and return to the Kamyaka forest.

The Bridge of Arrows

Arjuna gazed at the rippling waves of the ocean, full of wonder. Its waters stretched on and on endlessly, it seemed. He was on a pilgrimage to expiate a promise he had inadvertently broken. It had been decided when they married Draupadi jointly, that she would spend one year with each of the five Pandavas and the others could not invade their privacy. Arjuna had entered Yudhishthira's room by mistake, not realising that Draupadi was there. He had to embark on a year-long pilgrimage to atone.

Now he had reached the southernmost tip of the country – Rameshwaram.

He could not help but recall all the stories about Lord Rama that he had heard so often. Rama had established a Shivalinga here, seeking the blessings of Shiva before his journey to Lanka to rescue his wife Sita. Arjuna had visited the temple and prayed to Shiva as well.

As he gazed at the sea, he noticed the remnants of the bridge constructed by Rama's army of monkeys and bears that made it possible for them to cross over to Lanka.

A strange thought entered his mind. 'Lord Rama was a god in human form and one of the greatest archers of all time,' he mused aloud. 'I wonder why he asked monkeys, bears and even little squirrels to make a bridge out of sticks and stones? He could have built a bridge of arrows in the blink of an eye.'

There were several other pilgrims standing nearby who heard him, but none of them could come up with an answer.

Then Arjuna heard a shrill voice say, 'You look like a warrior. Perhaps you are a skilled archer. But you forget one thing. Would any bridge made of arrows be strong enough to bear the weight of the great monkey warriors like Sugreeva, Nala, Neela, Angada and Hanuman, who were in Rama's army?'

Arjuna turned around and was astonished to find that it was a small monkey speaking. 'In fact,' the monkey continued, 'small as I am, a bridge of arrows is likely to collapse if I step on it.'

Arjuna burst out laughing. 'I mean no disrespect, sir,' he said. 'But do you know what you're talking about? A bridge of arrows, constructed by a master archer, is as strong as one made of stone and wood.'

'All right,' said the monkey, 'since you sound so confident about this, I challenge you to prove your point. You build the bridge and I'll walk across it. If it does not collapse under my weight, you win.'

Arjuna didn't know whether to laugh or fly into a rage. That a small, shrivelled-looking monkey should challenge him, the greatest archer of his age! It was unthinkable! But all living beings had to be given a chance to express their views, so he tried to keep his cool.

'Agreed,' he replied as calmly as he could. 'Perhaps you are not aware that I am Arjuna, one of the five Pandavas, and I have been trained in the art of archery by none other than the legendary guru Dronacharya himself. I will prove my point. And I swear to you, if my bridge is unable to support your weight, I will light my own funeral pyre and enter it.'

'Agreed!' said the monkey.

Arjuna strung his bow, the mighty Gandiva, and let loose a flight of arrows that stretched far across the wide ocean. He added more and more till a solid looking bridge was created.

'Come, sir,' he said to the monkey with a satisfied smile. 'Is this bridge good enough for you? Look at the way I have meshed the arrows together. Please would you care to place your foot on it? I assure you, it is quite safe. You will not tumble into the ocean.'

'Let's see.' The monkey smiled back. But he did not step on to the bridge. Chanting 'Jai Rama, Jai Rama!', he placed only his long tail on it.

Arjuna went pale with shock. Before his eyes, his skilfully constructed bridge fell apart. 'How is this possible?' he exclaimed, as he watched his expertly placed arrows float away, tossed hither and thither by the waves.

'You've seen that it is. Would you like another chance?' the monkey cackled. 'A great archer like you deserves one more. Maybe some of the arrows were not strong enough.'

Arjuna felt the heat of the sun strongly on his brow. He wiped the sweat off, then took a deep breath. He was deeply shaken. To be defeated by a puny old monkey! He had shot as efficiently as he always did. His concentration had been as perfect as ever, his eye as keen, his arrows the best. Why did the bridge collapse? Somehow, he pulled himself together again. This fiasco would not be repeated, he vowed. His bridge would hold this time.

'Thanks for your kind consideration, sir,' he said, with folded hands.

He pulled at the Gandiva with all his strength. Arrow after arrow zoomed through the air, each fitting neatly into the preceding one. His speed was so great that the first row had barely formed before the second began to close with the third and the fourth following swiftly after. Row after row of arrows formed a huge bridge across the ocean that looked as unbreakable as a shaft of solid granite.

When the bridge was complete, with a low bow, he invited the monkey to test it. Once again, the monkey began to chant Rama's name: 'Jai Rama, Jai Rama!' as he stepped on to the bridge. He had barely completed ten paces when the bridge began to crumble. The agile monkey leapt off and landed safely on the shore.

Numb with shock and humiliation, Arjuna watched the waves carry his handiwork away once again.

All his expertise in archery was useless, he thought miserably. He could not even build a bridge that could support a frail little monkey. His shame overwhelmed him so greatly that he almost sank to the ground. Life was not really worth living now, he felt.

'You win, sir,' he said in a choked voice. 'I will fetch some wood for a pyre.'

Miserably, Arjuna began to search for driftwood on the shore of the ocean and stack it for his funeral pyre. He thought miserably of the dedication with which he had been preparing for the great battle with his cousins. But he had proved himself incapable of this minor deed.

Just as he was preparing to light the pyre and enter it, a young man who was passing by stopped to watch. 'What are you doing?' he asked. 'Why are you building this fire?'

Arjuna narrated the story of the bet and his ignominious defeat. 'The two of you had made a bet,' the young man said. 'But this is not the way it is done. There has to be an impartial referee to decide who wins and who loses. Do not throw away your life like this. If both of you agree, you should try again and I will judge your contest.'

'All right,' said the monkey. 'But wait and see, the outcome will be the same.'

Arjuna was quaking inwardly. This was his last chance to save himself. Before stringing his bow, he prayed fervently to Lord Krishna for help. Then he used all his powers of concentration and his skill to shoot each arrow.

Once again, a solid-looking bridge spanned the great ocean. Heart beating rapidly, Arjuna stepped back and requested the monkey to test it.

Having worsted Arjuna twice, the monkey had become so confident that he jumped on to the bridge with a smirk, completely forgetting to invoke Rama. To his surprise, the bridge stood firm. Unconvinced, he jumped up and down to test it further. But the bridge did not fall apart. The monkey took huge leaps, coming down with greater force each time. And soon, he had crossed the whole bridge without a single arrow getting dislodged from its place! The monkey was not ready to give up, though. To Arjuna's astonishment, his body began to expand.

Arjuna's eyes almost popped out as he saw the monkey grow larger and larger till he became as tall as a mountain. And then he realised that this monkey was none other than the great Hanuman himself.

Overwhelmed, Arjuna bowed low before Hanuman. If only he had realized whom he was competing against, he thought! As he knelt on the ground, Hanuman continued to test the bridge, stamping on it with such force that Arjuna expected it to crumble to pieces any minute. But to his delighted surprise, the bridge could withstand Hanuman's weight even in his gigantic form. As he watched anxiously, hoping the bridge would hold, Hanuman stepped off it with a baffled look on his face.

'I accept defeat,' he said. 'But there is a greater force than your arrows holding it together. The bridge acquired this invincible quality only after our judge came on the scene. I wonder who this young man is.'

A smile appeared on the young man's face and before their eyes he was transformed into Lord Vishnu himself. Overcome with awe, both Arjuna and Hanuman prostrated themselves before him.

'I am both Rama and Krishna,' he said, raising his hand in blessing. Then he turned to the Pandava, saying, 'Arjuna, you are unparalleled as an archer. Why do you think the bridge of arrows you created with such great skill did not hold up the first two times?'

Arjuna hung his head. 'Perhaps because I was too full of pride at my own abilities,' he said humbly. 'The third time I prayed to you before shooting the first arrow and your divine blessings added the needed strength to the bridge. Strength that could carry the weight of the mighty Hanuman even in his largest form.'

Hanuman folded his hands and knelt in front of Vishnu. 'I think, Lord, that I could not break the bridge the third time because in my overconfidence I forgot to call on your name, the way I did on the first two occasions. I was so full of myself that I thought I could succeed without asking for your blessings. Thank you, Lord, for coming here to show us the way and granting us this vision.'

'I too am full of gratitude to you, Lord, for granting this wisdom to us,' Arjuna added. 'I have made a discovery that I will remember all my life – that all power, all talent flows from the divine. I pray that you will forgive me for my arrogance.'

'You are both very dear to me,' Lord Vishnu replied. 'And I have already forgiven you. But before I go, there is something more I would like to say, Hanuman. Out of your devotion to Rama, you wanted to teach Arjuna a lesson for questioning his method of constructing the Rama Setu. But why did you accept a bet that would force him to take his own life? That was totally against the code of righteous conduct that you normally follow.'

Hanuman sighed. 'I am extremely ashamed I got carried away to that extent. That action, too, came from my desire to display my strength. I hope you will forgive me, dear Arjuna. I must make amends for this.'

'Only a noble being like you would acknowledge their mistake so humbly. Hanuman. You know that a great war is coming,' Lord Vishnu said, gently. 'A war between the forces of justice and injustice – the Pandavas and the Kauravas. That is where you can make amends – by helping the Pandavas.'

'You are absolutely right, Lord,' Hanuman said. 'Thanks for suggesting it. My dear Arjuna, this incident has bound us together in a way we could hardly have imagined. You have won my undying friendship. I promise to protect your chariot in the great war by being present on your banner.'

'Well said, Hanuman,' Lord Vishnu blessed them both again. 'With your presence on his banner, Arjuna will be invincible.'

Vishnu disappeared as miraculously as he had arrived. Hanuman and Arjuna stood still for a moment as they absorbed the miracle that had occurred. This event had made an enormous impact on both of them. Then they took leave of each other, embracing affectionately. As Arjuna watched Hanuman go, he felt suffused with hope and a new energy. He had made an important ally, who could swing the course of fortune in favour of the Pandavas in the coming war.

The Enchanted Pool

It was the twelfth year of the Pandavas' exile – the last before they had to go into hiding. They were getting quite restless by now. So, along with Draupadi, the five brothers decided to return to the forest of Dwaitavana for a change of scene.

The Pandavas had settled down into their new routine, when one day, an agitated brahmin arrived at their hut with a strange request. 'Kind princes, I beg you to help me,' he said, with folded hands. 'A terrible calamity has befallen me. I was preparing to set up my sacrificial fire when a deer wandered in from the forest. It began rubbing itself against my fire kindling sticks and before I could do anything, the sticks got entangled in its horns. This threw the animal into a panic. First it shook its head violently to dislodge them, then bounded off, trying to throw the sticks off. Please, brave ones, can you help find that deer and recover my sticks? I will be indebted to you forever.'

This was indeed a calamity because without the kindling sticks, which the forest dwellers used to light a fire, life could not go on. The brahmin would not be able to light his sacrificial fire and conduct his daily rituals, nor would he be able to cook food.

The brothers sprang up at once when they heard this. 'Do not worry,' Yudhishthira reassured the man. 'The deer could not have travelled far. We will recover your kindling sticks without delay.'

The Pandavas ran swiftly through the narrow forest paths, negotiating their way through low-hanging tree branches, and parting the dense bushes that obstructed their path. Soon, they caught sight of the deer, leaping and bounding a little ahead of them. They stepped up their pace, but no matter how fast they ran, the animal managed to stay just a little ahead of them.

Somewhat frustrated, Arjuna used all his strength to achieve a tremendous burst of speed and came very close to the deer. 'I've got it!' he cried, reaching out to catch hold of the animal. To his astonishment, before he could lay hands on it, the deer melted into thin air.

All five brothers halted in their tracks and stood there for a moment, completely stunned. 'How did that happen?' Bhima exclaimed, scratching his head. 'You almost had him in your grasp.'

'I just can't understand how. I'm as puzzled as you!' Arjuna's brow knotted in an uneasy frown.

‘It has to be an enchanted deer,’ Yudhishthira said, brushing the sweat off his brow. ‘No ordinary deer could vanish like that. I’m afraid someone has lured us here.’

Nakula slumped to the ground, totally demoralized. ‘This is what we’ve descended to,’ he said. ‘We can’t even help out a brahmin who appealed to us to solve a minor problem. Why is our fate dragging us down? We have always tried to do the right thing, always stayed true to the path of dharma. Why has this happened to us?’

‘Dear brother, when calamities descend, the only thing to do is bear them with fortitude,’ Yudhishthira said gently. ‘It is no use trying to search for explanations.’

‘I know why this is happening to us,’ Bhima averred. ‘It is because I did not kill that wretch Dussashana when he humiliated Draupadi and dragged her into the assembly hall. I neglected my duties.’

‘You are right, Bhima,’ Arjuna nodded in agreement. ‘I stayed silent when Karna, that lowborn son of a charioteer, insulted our beloved Draupadi with such vile language. Those foul words pierced me through and through and yet I let that evil one live. That is why we are in this pathetic state.’

‘And I neglected to slay that villainous Shakuni when he was deceiving us in that fateful game of dice,’ Sahadeva added, hanging his head. ‘I knew he was cheating but sat through it without protesting. Now we have to suffer the consequences.’

Yudhishthira was alarmed to see his brothers in this state of utter despair. He had to break this chain of self-recrimination somehow, or else the matter might reach a point of no return. Not only were they demoralized, all five were exhausted, hungry and thirsty. He needed to get them on their feet and involved in some course of action to snap out of this mood.

'Whatever it may be, right now I'm dying of thirst,' he said to Nakula. 'Can you climb that tree, brother, and try to catch sight of a pool or river nearby?'

Ever attentive to his elder brother's needs, Nakula immediately scrambled up the tree. After peering into the distance, he exclaimed, 'I can see some water hyacinths and cranes to the east. There must be some kind of water body there.'

'Well done!' Yudhishthira cried. 'Now please can you go there and fetch some water for us to drink?'

'Right away,' Nakula said and sprinted off nimbly.

After covering a short distance, he reached the place that he had spotted from the tree and was delighted to find a pool of crystal-clear water there. He himself was completely parched, so he decided to take a long drink before filling his quiver with water to carry back to his brothers. But as soon as he bent down and dipped a hand in the water, he heard a voice call out to him.

'Don't be in such a hurry, son of Madri,' someone said. 'This pool belongs to me. Before you take a single sip of water from it, you have to answer my questions.'

Nakula was taken aback. He looked all around, but he could not see anyone at all. His thirst was so overpowering that he could not bear to wait any longer. So he crouched near the pool, scooped up water in his cupped hands and drank deeply. The moment he gulped it down, a peculiar drowsiness overcame him. Immediately, he slumped to the ground and within a few minutes he had turned lifeless.

His brothers were waiting impatiently for him to return. When a long time passed and there was no sign of Nakula, they became concerned. 'Sahadeva, why don't you go and find out what is keeping our brother,' Yudhishthira said. 'It is unlike him to take so long.'

Sahadeva's anxiety about Nakula hastened his footsteps. When he caught sight of some cranes from a distance, he broke into a run and soon reached the pool.

It was a lovely spot, shaded with low-hanging trees and flowering bushes. He looked all around for Nakula and when his eyes fell on his limp frame stretched out on the ground, he started with shock. He bent to touch Nakula's body, then made a futile attempt to lift him up.

'Oh, my beloved brother, what has happened to you?' he lamented, when he realized Nakula was not breathing. 'Who could be responsible for this dastardly deed?' To find out what fatal blow could have felled Nakula, feverishly, he checked his body for wounds. To his astonishment, there was no sign of injury. Sahadeva rose, and ran an uneasy look over his surroundings, but all seemed calm and peaceful. There was no one to be seen, no armed men, not a single animal or monster. He thought of investigating further, but an unbearable thirst was tormenting him, so he decided to drink some water first.

'Wait a minute, Sahadeva,' a voice rang out, the moment he bent down to drink. 'This happens to be my pool. You cannot slake your thirst till you answer my questions.'

Sahadeva became alert immediately. He stood up and looked all around. But there was not a soul to be seen. Wondering if he might have imagined the voice, like his brother, he too ignored the warning. He filled his quiver and gulped down the water hurriedly. Within minutes, he also fell down dead.

The other three Pandavas kept waiting for the two brothers to return with the water. But time went by and there was no sign of either Nakula or Sahadeva.

'What is keeping Nakula and Sahadeva?' Bhima grumbled. 'Don't they realize that we are dying of thirst? Are they drinking up the whole pool?'

'You would have done that! Maybe they're taking a dip in the water to cool down after this tiring chase,' Arjuna said, trying to smile through dry lips.

Yudhishthira, however, frowned. 'They are not that irresponsible. I hope they did not meet with some kind of danger. Arjuna, please go and check on them. And do remember to fetch water for us, please.'

Arjuna rose at once and set off at a run, carrying his bow and quiver on his back. His thoughts were extremely troubled. There was something so mysterious about the way the deer vanished and now their two youngest brothers seemed to have disappeared too.

Was some enchantment being employed against them, he couldn't help wondering.

Then he realized that he had arrived at the pool. He let out a cry when he saw Nakula and Sahadeva lying lifeless on the ground. Thinking they might be sleeping, he tried to shake them awake. When he found that they remained limp and lifeless, his heart plummeted with horror. A stream of tears gushed from his eyes.

Utterly distraught, Arjuna sank to the ground and embraced the two cold bodies. 'What evil being did this to you, my brothers?' he lamented. 'I will make him suffer. To lose you in the prime of your youth! This is more than I can bear. Worse still, it looks as if you did not even have a chance to defend yourself like the warriors you are. But let me just get a drink of water from this pool first.'

Arjuna crouched near the pool to drink. The moment he had scooped up water in his hands, a voice called out: 'Halt, Arjuna! This pool belongs to me. You will have to answer my questions before you can drink. See what happened to your brothers. If you don't listen to me, you will meet the same fate.'

Arjuna leapt up in a fury. 'Come out of hiding, you coward, and face me like a man!' he shouted with rage. 'I will make quick work of you!' He swiftly let loose a volley of arrows in the direction of the sound.

Mocking laughter was all he received in response. 'Your arrows cannot find me,' the voice rang out scornfully. 'All you need to do is answer my questions. Then you can drink as deeply as you please.'

'I'm too thirsty to wait,' Arjuna muttered, and quickly took a long drink from the pool.

Within minutes, he met the same fate as his brothers and fell on the ground beside them.

By this time, Bhima and Yudhishthira were beginning to get extremely anxious. Each moment weighed on them heavily as they peered through the trees, waiting for the others.

'I fear something terrible has happened to our brothers,' Yudhishthira wrung his hands in despair. 'Even the doughty warrior Arjuna has not returned. Dear Bhima, can you go and see what's wrong? And please be careful. We are in the grip of misfortune so you need to be on your guard. And please bring back some water. I feel faint with thirst now.'

'Don't worry, dear brother, I'll bring them all back safe and sound,' Bhima proclaimed.

He got to his feet and set off, taking huge strides to reach the pool as soon as he could.

When he got there and caught sight of his brothers lying there lifeless, he let out a bellow of rage. 'Who slaughtered you in this foul manner? Most likely, it was Yakshas. These beings haunt forests and pools. But why my innocent brothers? All they wanted was a drink of water. I will not spare the killers. But first I must quench my thirst ...'

He had just stepped into the pool when a voice rang out: 'Heed my warning, Bhima! I am the guardian of this pool. You cannot drink till you answer my questions.'

'Try stopping me!' Bhima yelled back. He took huge mouthfuls and gulped the water down greedily. Immediately, he found the strength ebbing from his body. He barely had time to drag himself to the shore before he too fell down dead next to his brothers.

Now Yudhishthira was left all alone. As time slipped away and even Bhima did not return, his anxiety reached agonizing heights. 'Has some powerful person cursed them?' he wondered. 'Or are they wandering through the forest in search of water, crazed with thirst? Have they died or fainted? Oh, my beloved brothers, how I wish I hadn't sent you on this accursed quest!'

There was no choice left but to go search for them now. Besides, he too was so parched that he was ready to collapse. So, he set off in the direction of the pool. Yudhishthira trudged through the forest, encountering herds of spotted deer, wild boar and enormous birds till he arrived at a beautiful meadow. The meadow was carpeted with lush green, velvety grass and sprinkled with numerous multi-coloured wildflowers. Yudhishthira's eyes lit up at the sight of a pool of clear water in the middle of the meadow. Then his gaze fell on the lifeless forms of his brothers.

Yudhishthira's elation vanished immediately. He wept aloud, utterly devastated. He sat down beside them and mourned, caressing their still, cold faces: 'Had our vows to end like this? Did this misfortune have to strike just when our years of exile were almost over? What an accursed creature I am! Even the gods have turned against me.'

He paused to wipe his tears, gazing at the strong, muscular frames of his four brothers. 'O Nakula and Sahadeva, I can't understand how my heart is still in one piece. It should have shattered to pieces seeing you and dear Bhima and Arjuna dead. There is nothing left to live for any more ...'

However, as he sat there, totally dispirited, the mystery of their sudden demise continued to bother him. His brothers were among the most invincible warriors of their time. He could not help wondering what kind of calamity could have befallen them, one after the other. There were no wounds on their bodies, no footprints, no indications of any kind of struggle. Was some magical force responsible for their deaths? Maybe Duryodhana had poisoned the pool ...

As he looked at the water, he realized that his thirst was quite unbearable now.

So, Yudhishthira too succumbed and entered the pool to take a long drink.

Once again, the disembodied voice was heard: 'Listen, Yudhishthira, your brothers lost their lives because they did not pay attention to my words. If you do not heed me, you will follow them. I am the owner of this pool. You have to answer my questions before you drink from it.'

A sudden light burst upon Yudhishthira. This was a Yaksha – the guardian of this pool speaking. It could be the answer to the riddle of his brothers' mysterious deaths. Hope sparked in Yudhishthira's heart. Maybe all was not lost, he thought.

'Greetings, sir,' he replied, bowing politely. 'Please go ahead and ask your questions. I will be only too happy to answer them.'

The words were barely out of his mouth when the Yaksha began to fire questions at Yudhishthira in quick succession, scarcely giving him time to think.

'Listen carefully before you answer,' he began. 'Tell me, what makes the sun rise and set?'

'It's the power of Lord Brahma,' Yudhishthira replied immediately.

'What helps a man in a dangerous situation?' The next question followed at once.

'It is courage that comes to a man's aid when he is in danger,' Yudhishthira was quick to reply.

'Which science must a man study in order to acquire wisdom?' asked the Yaksha.

'A man does not become wise simply by studying the classics. Keeping company with those who have acquired wisdom also makes one wise,' Yudhishthira answered confidently.

'Who is it that nurtures a human being more selflessly than even the earth we live upon?' asked the Yaksha.

'It is the mother. A mother who nurtures her children with great devotion is far nobler than the earth,' Yudhishthira replied.

'Hmm…' the Yaksha murmured. 'You seem to know many of the right answers. But tell me, who is considered higher even than the heavens?'

'A responsible and kind father possesses a stature higher than the heavens,' was Yudhishthira's swift response.

'All right, do you know what is faster than the wind?' the Yaksha did not waste any time in posing the next question.

Yudhishthira answered just as quickly, 'The human mind. Its motion is much faster than the wind.'

'True … but what can be worse than the condition of a shrivelled straw?' asked the Yaksha.

'A man beset with worries is far more pitiable than a piece of shrivelled straw,' said Yudhishthira.

'And who do you think is the best friend a traveller can have?' The Yaksha fired his next question.

'Learning is the best friend a traveller can have,' the answer was already on Yudhishthira's lips.

'Then tell me, who is the best friend a man can have when he is at home?' was the next poser.

'Obviously, it is a man's wife who is his best friend at home,' Yudhishthira responded with a smile.

'Talking of friends, who is the best friend of one who is ill, and of one who is about to die?' asked the Yaksha.

'A physician is the best friend of one who is sick and charity the friend of a dying man,' Yudhishthira said gravely.

'Who accompanies a man after his death?' was the next question.

'Dharma is the only companion that goes with a man's soul after he is dead,' Yudhishthira said without hesitating.

'All right. Do you know which is the biggest vessel in existence?' questioned the Yaksha.

'The earth, because it contains all,' Yudhishthira replied.

'You are a knowledgeable man, indeed. Do you know how an individual can find happiness?' asked the Yaksha next.

'The only way a person can find true happiness is by pursuing good conduct.' Yudhishthira did not waste even a second in replying.

'Which quality should one renounce to be loved by one and all?' the tricky Yaksha brought up another poser.

Yudhishthira replied, 'Pride. Only by abandoning pride does a person become lovable.'

The Yaksha was ready with one more question. 'What kind of loss brings joy rather than sorrow?'

'The loss of anger,' Yudhishthira answered without a moment's hesitation.

'Tell me, is there any kind of loss that makes a man wealthy?' the Yaksha asked next.

'The loss of desire. It is by renouncing desire that a man acquires true wealth,' Yudhishthira replied instantly.

The Yaksha asked then, 'Who is a real brahmin? One who is born a brahmin, one who is learned, or one who pursues the path of righteous conduct?'

'Birth does not make you a true brahmin, neither does learning. A man might be well versed in all the four Vedas, but if he does not pursue righteous conduct, he cannot be called a brahmin,' was Yudhishthira's reply.

The Yaksha was ready with another set of questions, 'Which enemy is invincible? What constitutes an incurable disease? And what makes a man noble or ignoble?'

Yudhishthira responded, 'Anger is the invincible enemy. Covetousness is an incurable disease. He who desires the well-being of all creatures is truly noble, and one who has no mercy is ignoble.'

The Yaksha was not done yet. 'What is the greatest wonder in the world?' was his next question.

'The greatest wonder is that each day men see people depart this world for Yama's abode. Yet those who are alive wish they could live forever. What greater wonder can there be?' Yudhishthira said sagely.

In this manner, the Yaksha continued to test Yudhishthira with all kinds of tricky questions. The oldest of the Pandava brothers remained undaunted and continued to reply without hesitating.

Finally, the Yaksha said, 'You have answered all my questions correctly, O king. As a reward, I will grant you a boon. One of your brothers can be brought back to life. Whom do you choose?'

Yudhishthira paused to think for a moment, then he said, 'Please revive the handsome lotus-eyed and broad-chested Nakula, who lies prostrate like a felled tree.'

'Why did you choose Nakula?' asked the Yaksha. 'You could have chosen the mighty Bhima. They say he is dearest to you among all your brothers. You could have even chosen Arjuna, whose skill in wielding arms is unparalleled. Both are your real brothers and either of them could have protected you better against your enemies than Nakula.'

'It is dharma and dharma alone that protects a man, O Yaksha, not physical strength or expertise in weapons,' Yudhishthira said without a moment's hesitation. 'When a man abandons dharma, he has chosen the path to destruction. My mother Kunti can find consolation in the fact that at least one of her sons is alive – me. It is only just that my stepmother Madri should also receive that comfort if her son Nakula is revived.'

'You are truly the epitome of dharma, Yudhishthira,' the Yaksha said approvingly. 'You have pleased me greatly with your choice. Pleased me so much that I will bring all your brothers back to life.'

And before Yudhishthira's astonished eyes, one by one all four of his brothers sat up and rose to their feet. They stared at each other in surprise. A tearful reunion followed when they learned how they had recovered from their mysterious ordeal. The younger Pandavas fell at Yudhishthira's feet and thanked him profusely for saving their lives.

But before they began to share their stories, Yudhishthira folded his hands to the invisible Yaksha. 'I am extremely grateful to you, O Yaksha,' he said. 'Will you grant me one more favour? Will you let me see what you look like?'

'Granted,' said the Yaksha.

And suddenly a grotesque-looking being appeared before them. The eldest Pandava bowed deeply.

'You have done me a great honour, O Yaksha,' he was beginning to say, when his eyes widened in utter amazement. The Yaksha transformed into Yama, the god of death, Yudhishthira's own father.

'Dear son, I wanted to meet you and prepare you for the enormous test that lies ahead of you. So, I took the form of the deer as well as the Yaksha,' Yama explained as all five Pandavas stood there stunned. 'Your period of exile in the forest will end in a few days. Then only the thirteenth year of living incognito remains. That too will go by without any difficulty. I can confidently say that your enemies will not be able to get the better of you.'

Then he embraced Yudhishthira and blessed him and his younger brothers.

The Pandavas made their way back to Dwaitavana, discussing the strange experience. Arjuna had returned from his father Indra's abode, greatly empowered. Bhima's strength had multiplied tenfold when he met his brother Hanuman during his quest for the saugandhika flower.

This happened when Arjuna left to obtain the divine weapons from Indra. The rest of the family went to stay at Badri ashram. One day the wind wafted a beautiful blue saugandhika flower into Draupadi's hands. When Draupadi longed for some more, Bhima set off through the forest, following the scent the wind had spread. But on the way, he found a huge old monkey blocking the path. When Bhima asked him to move aside, the monkey said he was too old to get up and suggested that Bhima jump over him. Bhima said it would be disrespectful, so the monkey told him to lift his tail and pass. The powerful Bhima tried to hold up the tail, but despite all his efforts, the tail would not budge. Then he realised this could not be an ordinary monkey. He apologised humbly and asked the monkey to reveal himself only to discover that he was his brother Hanuman, the son of Vayu. Hanuman's divine form dazzled Bhima. Then Hanuman pulled Bhima into a deep embrace to enhance his strength and promised to provide support at the great battle that was imminent. He pointed the way to the pond where the saugandhika flowers grew and left.

And now, Yudhishthira too had acquired a heavenly lustre after his encounter with his father Yama.

Arjuna's Charioteer

The Pandavas decided to spend the last year of their exile in the court of King Virata, the ruler of Matsya, adopting different disguises. Virata was known as a kindly person and his wealth lay in his vast herds of cattle. Yudhishthira assumed the garb of a sanyasi and won the king's favour with his knowledge of astrology and the scriptures. He took the name Kanka and claimed to be proficient in the game of dice.

Bhima used his skill in the culinary arts to take up the job of a cook and called himself Valala. Arjuna, heedful of Urvashi's curse, dressed in women's garments and passed off as a eunuch known as Brihannala, and taught singing and dancing to the ladies of the court. Draupadi served as Sairandhari, and was a companion to the queen and other ladies, dressing their hair and engaging in pleasant conversation.

Nakula, with his skill in horse riding and the equestrian arts, decided to work in the stable under the name Damagranthi, while Sahadeva took on the task of a keeper of the cowshed, calling himself Tantripala.

The thirteenth year went by in this manner.

The year was reaching its end, but Duryodhana had been searching for them and became suspicious that the Pandavas might be hiding in Virata's court. To force them to reveal themselves, he sent an army to steal Virata's cattle. Virata's son Uttar Kumar went to fight the Kauravas and Arjuna, disguised as Brihannala, acted as his charioteer to protect the young man. Arjuna routed the Kaurava army but asked Uttar to keep his secret and claim the victory for himself.

After such a long wait, it was finally time for the Pandavas to shed their disguise. When Uttar also disclosed the truth about the battle, the grateful Virata offered his throne to Yudhishthira and his daughter Uttara to Arjuna in marriage. Arjuna, however, suggested that she marry his son Abhimanyu, because he looked upon her as a daughter.

Yudhishthira too refused Virata's throne and the Pandavas left his court to live in Upaplavya, a city in his kingdom of Matsya.

They sent word about this to their friends and well-wishers. Soon Krishna, Balarama, Subhadra, Abhimanyu, Drupada, Shikhandin, Drishtadyumna and Draupadi's sons arrived at Upaplavya along with the Yadava princes.

Abhimanyu was Arjuna's son from his wife Subhadra, who was Krishna's sister. He was a handsome young man, highly skilled in the art of war and everybody's favourite. It was said he was the son of Chandradev, the moon god, who had sent him to earth for a short time.

The joyful reunion was followed by the grand celebration of Abhimanyu and Uttara's wedding.

Once the festivities were over, a meeting was held to take counsel for the future course of action.

The consensus was that every effort should be made to avoid a conflict, even though all the participants in the discussion were fully aware that Duryodhana would never agree to an amicable settlement. As a first step, an emissary was sent to the Kaurava court, asking them to return the Pandavas' kingdom peaceably.

At the same time, foreseeing a conflict, both Pandavas and Kauravas began to approach the powerful rulers of the land to seek alliances with them.

After meeting the Pandavas, Krishna had returned to Dwarka. Arjuna decided to go there to ask for his help in the forthcoming battle.

Meanwhile, Duryodhana was not sitting idle either. His spies had kept him well informed about everything that was going on at the Pandavas' end. Hearing that Arjuna was heading towards Dwarka, he had his swiftest horses harnessed to his chariot and sped towards Krishna's kingdom.

It so happened that both cousins arrived in Dwarka at the same time. When they reached, they were informed that Krishna was fast asleep. The matter of an alliance with Krishna was extremely urgent for

Arjuna and Duryodhana. Given their close relationship with Krishna, both possessed the privilege of entering his bed chamber unhindered.

Thus, they entered Krishna's room almost at each other's heels. Duryodhana flung a dark look at Arjuna and quickly occupied the seat next to Krishna's head. He placed himself on it grandly, as if the highly ornamented chair that looked like a throne was the right place for him. Arjuna folded his hands in greeting to his cousin. He decided to stand at Krishna's feet respectfully.

After some time, Krishna opened his eyes. His gaze fell on Arjuna first since he stood directly opposite him. His face lit up and he greeted the Pandava warmly.

This did not please Duryodhana at all. 'Greetings, Krishna,' he said sulkily. 'I am here too, waiting for you.'

'Welcome, Duryodhana,' Krishna replied. 'What a pleasure to see both of you! But for what reason have the two of you honoured me with a visit? And what urgency made you wait here, right in my bedroom?'

'I am sure you know that our cousins have returned and are demanding the kingdom Yudhishthira lost in the game of dice.' Duryodhana's voice was bitter with spite. 'We cannot let them take what is ours by right. You well know what this means. War. All-out war!'

Krishna nodded gravely and cast a look at Arjuna, but Arjuna remained silent.

Duryodhana started off again. 'We have both come to request your support. Krishna, we are equally close in relationship and equally dear to you. You cannot say that one of us is closer than the other. But the fact is, I arrived here before Arjuna. According to our traditions, in such a situation, the person who arrives first has the prior claim. You are the pillar of righteous conduct. Your actions serve as an example to others. Please keep in mind that I was the first to enter your room.'

'Dear Duryodhana, I do not deny that you arrived first,' Krishna said gently. 'However, Arjuna was the one I saw first. So, you see, his claim on my support is equal to yours. For this reason, I am dividing my resources into two. Now you know that the Narayanas, my tribesmen, are formidable warriors. Their skill in weapons is such that they are invincible in battle. On one side, I place the vast army of the Narayanas and on the other, I offer myself, completely unarmed. And Duryodhana, since you are laying stress on the importance of maintaining traditional values, please keep in mind that when favours are being granted, customarily it is the younger person who gets the first choice.'

Krishna turned to Arjuna and said. 'You have to decide what you prefer. Take your time and think over it, since this choice would be crucial. Would you prefer to take me, alone and without any weapons, or would you rather have the support of the vast host of the Narayanas? Let us know, Arjuna.'

Arjuna replied immediately. 'I don't need to think over it,' he said humbly. 'My mind is made up. I'd rather have you on our side, even if you will not wield any weapons.'

When he heard this, Duryodhana's joy knew no bounds. 'What a fool Arjuna is,' he thought privately. Aloud he said, 'Krishna, Arjuna has made his choice. I willingly accept the support of the Narayanas.' Saying this, he rose hastily to take his leave.

Duryodhana was impatient to go back to Hastinapur and share what he thought was his triumph over the Pandavas. But he wanted to meet Krishna's brother Balarama, and ask for his support too.

After he had gleefully narrated the story of Arjuna's choice, he said, 'Balarama, you have always been fair and objective. You know that right is on our side. I request you to pledge your support to the Kauravas in the forthcoming battle.'

Balarama's brow knotted. 'I have always been impartial in my dealings with you and the Pandavas,' he replied in measured tones, as if choosing his words carefully. 'I also keep reminding Krishna that both the Kauravas and the Pandavas are equally close to us. However, if Arjuna has asked Krishna to support his side, I am sorry, but I cannot join you, Duryodhana. I give you my word that I will not join Arjuna either. There is one thing, however, that I want to emphasise: if war should erupt, I exhort you to abide by the kshatriya code of conduct. Your great ancestors attached much importance to following it and this is what won them the respect of all the rulers of this land.'

Duryodhana's face fell when Balarama refused to pledge his support. 'I am deeply disappointed,' he said. 'But at least Krishna has offered me the Narayanas. Farewell, Balarama. Please remember to abide by your promise that you will not side with my cousins.'

When Duryodhana left for Hastinapur, he was beside himself with excitement. 'What a coup!' he thought to himself. 'I always knew that Arjuna was completely brainless. What use is an unarmed Krishna without his army to support him in battle? I am also convinced that whatever he might say, in his heart of hearts, Balarama is also with us.'

When Duryodhana had departed, Krishna turned to Arjuna. 'Why did you make this choice?' he asked with a smile. 'Why did you prefer

me on your side, unarmed and even without my army? No one would consider this a wise decision, when such a great war awaits you.'

'Krishna, you have the power to face all the princes of the land in battle without the aid of weapons,' Arjuna answered, his face serious. 'I know this. And it has always been my secret ambition to someday equal your prowess in warfare. I long to win laurels in battle like you. I want to take on whole armies single-handed and somewhere I am confident that I will be able to do it. Please, will you stay beside me in this war? If you drive my chariot, I feel I can achieve what no warrior in our land has achieved till now.'

'So you are trying to emulate me?' Krishna's face was wreathed with smiles. He raised his hand in blessing and said, 'May you achieve your ambitions, Arjuna. I promise to be by your side and guide you through the course of this important war. I will drive your chariot.'

Arjuna bowed deeply and took his leave. His heart was brimming with hope and confidence because he knew that with Krishna by his side, he had nothing to fear in what would no doubt be a savage war against the Kauravas.

The Passing of Bhishma

Bhishma, the granduncle of the Pandavas and Kauravas, had suffered much because of the rivalry between them. His heart as well as his code of ethics made him conscious that the Pandavas had been unjustly treated. However, his oath of loyalty to the kingdom of Hastinapur did not allow him to do much more than offer advice to Dhritirashtra and his sons. Advice that was not usually taken.

The Pandavas had fulfilled the conditions imposed on them by Duryodhana after Yudhishthira lost the fateful game of dice. They had completed twelve years of exile in the forest and one year of living incognito. After taking counsel from all their well-wishers, their father-in-law King Drupada of Panchala sent a brahmin emissary to

Dhritirashtra on behalf of the Pandavas to request him to restore his nephews' share of the kingdom.

When Dhritirashtra heard about the arrival of the emissary, he welcomed him to his court. The man put forward his case eloquently, as he addressed the assembled elders and courtiers. 'The sons of Pandu have been deprived of their share of their father's kingdom,' he said to Dhritirashtra, Bhishma and the others. 'They have suffered much, but are ready to forgive all if their rights are restored. I appeal to your sense of justice and fair play. Do not delay in this matter, I beg you.'

Bhishma nodded in agreement. 'The gods have demonstrated their goodwill towards the Pandavas,' he said in measured tones. 'They have protected them through their long years of exile. This means that they have divine endorsement. Many powerful rulers support the five brothers too, because they believe their cause is just. Yet they are asking for peace. It would be the wise and correct thing to give back their kingdom to them.'

The moment he said this, Karna interrupted angrily, 'You are not telling us anything new, O brahmin! Yudhishthira lost his kingdom in the game of dice, so he cannot claim it now. If he wants it, he should beg for it on bended knee. In any case, the condition of spending the last year in exile incognito was not fulfilled. They should return to the forest.'

'You are speaking out of turn, Karna,' Bhishma admonished him. 'Imprudently as well. If we do not pay heed to King Drupada's messenger, we are inviting our destruction.'

Immediately, loud voices began to be raised in the assembly, each putting forward his opinion. Dhritirashtra realised he needed to intervene. He told Drupada's envoy, 'Kindly return to your kingdom and inform Yudhishthira that I am sending my trusted adviser Sanjaya to discuss this matter with him.'

Sanjaya was then despatched on a mission to make peace with the Pandavas. He addressed Yudhishthira with smooth words, praising his rectitude and trying to persuade him not to wage war on his cousins.

Yudhishthira gave patient ear to Sanjaya's exhortations. Then he said, 'Tell my respected uncle that he was good to us and offered us our share of the kingdom. Then his son drove us out using unfair means. My uncle crowned me king himself – does he want me to lead a beggarly existence now, living on the charity of other rulers? And please tell my cousin Duryodhana that he treated me like a slave, insulted my wife and deprived us of our inheritance. Yet, I have forgiven him all. We are five brothers. All we ask is five villages in the territory of Hastinapur so we can survive with honour.'

Sanjaya returned and reported Yudhishthira's message in Dhritirashtra's court. He also mentioned that Arjuna had announced that his Gandiva bow was eager to wage war.

Hearing this, both Bhishma and Vidura counselled the old king to be just and prudent. If he returned their kingdom to his nephews, he would avoid a destructive war and save his sons' lives. However, Duryodhana was adamant. He told his father that he was not willing to concede any territory at all to his cousins, not even a portion of land equal to the point of a needle.

Despite this, Krishna made one last attempt to persuade Duryodhana to right the old wrong. But even his words failed to have any effect. The misguided prince made a plan to capture Krishna instead, saying that once he was their prisoner, the Pandavas would be cowed into submission.

When he heard this, Krishna laughed out loud. His body began to glow with an unearthly radiance. And as all the assembled courtiers and sages watched awestruck, the Devas emerged from his body—Brahma on his forehead, Indra, Varuna, Kubera and Yama on his shoulders, the eleven Rudras on his chest. All the other gods were present too. The Pandavas, Balarama and other warriors surrounded him and his many arms held different weapons. The earth shook and Krishna's radiance blinded the terrified onlookers.

Then, taking pity on their plight, he resumed his human form and turned to leave. As he was mounting his chariot, he said, 'I have tried to avert this war, but Duryodhana is bent on his destruction.'

There was no option left for the Pandavas now, but to wage war. It was a difficult and painful choice for all of them.

On the first day, before the battle began, Yudhishthira removed his armour, laid down his weapons and walked towards the Kaurava masses, who were ready to attack. This action astonished all. The Kauravas thought he had lost his nerve and was suing for peace. But

Yudhishthira was headed towards the place where his granduncle Bhishma stood.

He bent low before the venerable elder and touched his feet. 'Grandsire,' he said with great respect, 'please grant us permission to begin the battle. We have taken the audacious step to face you in these hostilities. I beg you to bless us before we begin to hurl weapons at each other.'

'My son,' Bhishma replied, 'you have always followed the code of righteous conduct, maintaining the tradition of the descendants of Bharata. You have my blessings. I know your cause is just and victory will be yours. I am compelled to fight on the side of the Kauravas since I have sworn allegiance to Hastinapur, but my good wishes are with you.'

Yudhishthira then requested the other elders for their blessings and received them.

The great battle began. Bhishma was leading the Kaurava forces and, being a seasoned warrior, he inflicted terrible losses on the Pandava army every day. The Pandavas fought back with exceptional courage and decimated the ranks of Dhritirashtra's sons. Bhima, Arjuna and other great warriors wreaked havoc on the Kauravas.

However, whenever Arjuna came face to face with Bhishma, his resolution wavered. The strength of his bow weakened because he did not have the heart to inflict any wounds on his grandsire. Krishna, who was acting as his charioteer, exhorted him repeatedly but Arjuna just could not bring himself to battle Bhishma with the same fierceness with which he confronted his other opponents.

'This is war, Arjuna,' Krishna tried once more. 'Remember what I told you? You must put all your emotions aside and attend to the task at hand. Do you want to win or not? Remember what you have been through at Duryodhana's hands, remember Draupadi's brutal humiliation! Bhishma is your elder, but right now he is your enemy. Can't you understand that this weakness of yours is causing enormous setbacks to the Pandava side?'

Arjuna hung his head, then nodded. He understood what Krishna was trying to say. 'I will try and do as you advise, O Krishna,' he said faintly, ashamed of his weakness.

Just then Bhishma appeared before them, cutting down their soldiers with his ferocious blows. 'Now is the time, Arjuna,' Krishna whispered. But once again, Arjuna's hands lost their strength and his heart melted.

Krishna could not take it any longer. He jumped down from the chariot and cried, 'Arjuna if you do not act, I will be compelled to hurl my discus at Bhishma and finish him off myself!'

Arjuna ran after him, crying, 'No Krishna, no! Please don't break your promise! You had said you would not use any arms in this war. I will perform my duty, even if it is to kill my beloved granduncle.'

By chance, the course of battle carried Bhishma away as he turned to parry an attack from behind him.

Arjuna, however, had been jolted into the realisation that to save his cause, he had no choice but to target his own flesh and blood.

The great battle had raged for nine days now and many brave warriors had laid down their lives.

The tenth day arrived. Steeling himself, Arjuna entered the field and, according to plan, targeted Bhishma from behind Shikhandin. This warrior served in the court of Drupada and was actually the reincarnation of princess Amba, who had sworn to revenge herself on Bhishma for rejecting her in marriage. Bhishma had taken a vow not to fight Shikhandin, since he had been born a woman.

This made him an easy target. Shikhandin, driven by his sense of wrong, riddled the old man with arrows. Arjuna backed him with a steady hail of barbs. Harried in this manner, Bhishma was hard put to control himself from attacking Shikhandin. He stood stoically as the shafts surrounded him like a deadly cloud.

When Arjuna's onslaught penetrated the weak points in Bhishma's armour, he smiled. Turning to Dussashana, who was fighting next to him, Bhishma said, suppressing a groan, 'Ah … these arrows tear into my flesh like the claws of young crabs gouging their mother's body. They cannot come from Shikhandin's bow. They have to be from Arjuna's Gandiva.'

He seized a spear and threw it at Arjuna with all his force. Arjuna immediately countered it with three arrows that slashed it to pieces in mid-air. Bhishma tried to descend from his chariot, holding his sword and shield in an attempt to engage in a hand to hand combat with his grandnephew. Within seconds, Arjuna's arrows pierced his shield and splintered it to fragments. The old man was hurtled from his chariot, so completely riddled with arrows that not even an inch of bare space was visible between them on his body.

As the veteran warrior fell, the gods in the heavens folded their hands, to honour his greatness. They sent a shower of cooling rain over the battlefield, while a scented breeze wafted through the terrible melee, making the combatants pause and wonder.

In no time at all, the news had spread. 'Bhishma Pitamah has fallen!' was the wail that resounded amidst the clash of steel upon steel, the groans of the wounded and dying, the neighing of horses and trumpeting of elephants. The Kaurava forces felt their knees buckling as their courage ebbed at the loss of their mighty leader – Bhishma, the son of Ganga who had performed so many extraordinary deeds of valour. Bhishma, who had made the enormous sacrifice for the sake of his father's happiness.

All fighting halted, out of reverence to this legendary warrior. Bhishma lay on the arena, but his body remained suspended above the ground. The arrows that studded it completely made it impossible for him to rest on the ground. Men surrounded him, overcome at the sight of the man who was considered incomparable in the art of warfare now lying on a bed of arrows. A peculiar lustre emanated from his body and it seemed as if the blood that dripped from his wounds was a holy elixir, purifying the battlefield. Bhishma had done his duty with exemplary commitment. He had fought on Duryodhana's side because he had sworn fealty to them, even though his heart was with the Pandavas.

While the powerful rulers of the land stood with their heads bowed, in the heavens too, the gods stood around Lord Brahma.

'What can we do for you?' the men asked. 'How can we make you comfortable on this terrible bed?'

'All I need is some support for my head,' Bhishma said. His voice was still unwavering, despite the agony his wounds caused him. 'See how it's hanging down? It's very uncomfortable.'

Princes ran to fetch pillows of silk and brocade. But Bhishma waved them all away. 'It is very kind of you, but this is not what I require,' he said with a polite smile. 'Come forward, dear Arjuna. Please provide a cushion that befits an old warrior.'

Arjuna, who stood there with the others, mourning for his grandsire, understood at once. Immediately he removed three arrows from his quiver and placed them under Bhishma's head.

'Ah ... I feel much more comfortable now,' said Bhishma with a sigh. 'Noble rulers, I thank you for your concern. But Arjuna's arrows have given my head the proper support it needed. This pillow is just right. I will lie like this till the sun turns north. Only then will my soul leave my body. You can bid me farewell then – that is, those of you who survive the battle.'

Then Bhishma addressed Arjuna again. 'My son, my throat is completely parched. Can you get me some water to drink?'

Arjuna lifted his bow and drew the string taut. He let loose an arrow, aiming it at the earth on the right side of Bhishma. As the shaft pierced the earth, a jet of sweet water shot out of it and arched into the grandsire's mouth. The dying man drank deeply and was satisfied. People said that it was his mother Ganga herself, rising from the earth to quench her son's thirst.

'My dear Duryodhana,' Bhishma addressed the Kaurava prince, 'Did you observe Arjuna's feat? He brought water out of the earth with the force of his arrow. Is there any other man on earth who can do this? Please take my advice and end this war. Let there be peace between you when I leave this world.'

Duryodhana made no reply because the idea did not please him at all. He turned on his heel and left, along with the other kings, who made for their camps.

Afterwards, Karna, who had vowed not to take part in the battle while Bhishma was the supreme commander, came to pay his respects. Bhishma blessed him and told him to continue the fight using his expertise in weapons to the full extent.

Bhishma remained suspended on his bed of arrows till the end of the battle of Kurukshetra. His soul left his body only after he had given a discourse to Yudhishthira on the virtues of righteous conduct.

Abhimanyu Pierces the Chakravyuh

The great war continued to rage on the battlefields of Kurukshetra and many noble warriors met their end. On the tenth day, when the grandsire Bhishma himself fell because of Shikhandin, as foretold, a new commander-in-chief had to be appointed.

An anxious Duryodhana discussed the matter with his closest friend and confidante Karna. 'We have lost our most capable general, Karna,' he said. 'Bhishma Pitamah would certainly have led us to victory. I don't think there is anyone who can replace him, but we have to choose a head for our army immediately. Do you have any suggestions?' he asked.

'It is a difficult choice.' Karna's brow knotted in thought. 'All the monarchs and princes supporting us are great warriors, equal in strength and valour,' Karna said. 'If we select one of them as our leader, the others might feel slighted. This is most likely to affect their performance in battle. Why don't we ask Guru Dronacharya to take command? He is a highly skilled fighter, though he is not a kshatriya. However, he has been the guru of most of our allies and they all have great respect for him.'

'You speak wisely, dear Karna,' Duryodhana said. 'Let us request Dronacharya to be our leader.'

All the princes who supported the Kauravas were invited to assemble and Duryodhana made a formal request to Dronacharya. 'Respected guru,' he said, with folded hands, 'you stand tall amongst us, not only as a warrior unparalleled in the art of warfare, but also in your wisdom and knowledge of the arts and sciences. Now that our grandsire Bhishma has been laid low by Arjuna, I beg you to take over his position as the supreme commander of the Kaurava army.'

The princes gathered there acclaimed the proposal with loud cheers. Dronacharya accepted graciously, saying, 'You do me a great honour, Duryodhana. Rest assured, I will see to it that victory is ours.'

True to his word, the guru wasted no time and got busy planning his strategy.

In the meantime, Duryodhana and Karna got together with Dussashana to hatch a plot.

'I think it would be best to capture Yudhishthira alive rather than slay him in battle,' Duryodhana proposed.

'Are you sure?' Dussashana frowned. 'Won't it be better to finish all of them off?'

'I'm sure Duryodhana has a good reason for suggesting this,' Karna smiled as he stroked his moustache thoughtfully.

'I do,' Duryodhana nodded. 'Listen, if the oldest Pandava brother is slain, the others will flare up with thoughts of revenge. They will throw themselves into the battle even more fiercely and inflict heavy losses on us. However, if Yudhishthira is captured and made prisoner, we can play on his sentiments. You know how easy it is to manipulate him. Maybe we could even entice him into another game of dice, which he would no doubt lose.' Duryodhana burst into uproarious laughter and the other two joined in.

'What a master schemer you are, brother!' Dussashana cackled. 'I almost pity poor Yudhishthira.'

'I'd love to see the look on their faces when we accomplish this,' Karna said gleefully.

After discussing this matter further, Duryodhana approached Dronacharya. 'Respected guru, I'm sure you have drawn out an unbeatable strategy for the battle tomorrow. However, I would like to make a request,' he said. 'At this point, we feel it would be best to capture Yudhishthira alive. We are no longer interested in a complete victory over the Pandavas. If you can take Yudhishthira into your custody, we will be more than happy with your work as a commander.'

The guru's face lit up. The truth was, Drona's heart was not in the battle, deeply attached as he was to the Pandavas. Since he had sworn fealty to the court of Hastinapur, he had no choice but to fight on the side of the Kauravas. When he heard this, he was overjoyed. 'How can I bless you, dear Duryodhana!' he replied enthusiastically. 'It is heartwarming to know that you have no desire to slay your cousin Yudhishthira, who is the soul of righteousness. I can see now that your intentions are honourable. You plan to defeat the Pandavas, make peace with them and then return their kingdom to them. This is exactly what I want too. Truly the gods are pleased with Yudhishthira ... he has won even the hearts of his enemies.'

Duryodhana and the other two exchanged sly glances. How easily the guru had fallen into their trap!

Both sides had employed spies to keep themselves informed about the plans of their opponents. Thus, the news that Drona intended to capture Yudhishthira alive soon reached the Pandavas. The brothers realized that this was a serious threat. Drona was unparalleled in the art of warfare. Not only was he highly skilled in the use of arms, but he had knowledge of a vast variety of invincible secret weapons.

Even more alarming was the fact that when he made up his mind to achieve something, he would not give up till he had done it. If Guru Drona had promised Duryodhana that he would take Yudhishthira prisoner, he would not rest till he had accomplished the deed. This meant that extra precautions had to be taken to protect the eldest of the Pandavas. So, they decided on a battle formation that would prevent anyone from getting close to Yudhishthira.

The first day of Dronacharya's command was real torture for the Pandava forces. The general was everywhere, wreaking havoc like a destructive fire. He sliced through their army, cutting down warriors like grass. Along with the whizzing of arrows,the clash of steel, the yells of the soldiers and the cries of the wounded, many brutal encounters also took place.

A fierce duel was being fought between Sahadeva and Shakuni. After the treacherous game of dice and Draupadi's humiliation, Sahadeva had vowed to kill Shakuni. However, apart from his skill with dice, the Kauravas' uncle was also an expert in using weapons of illusion, like creating a fog to confound his opponents. This made the encounter more difficult, but Sahadeva was determined to fulfill his promise. When their chariots broke under the impact of their blows, they hit out at each other with maces. But Shakuni survived the day.

Nakula was doing battle with his uncle Salya, his mother Madri's brother, who had been tricked into supporting the Kauravas. Nakula managed to shatter his chariot and Salya had to retreat. Later, Salya came face to face with Bhima, who harried him so severely that the old man decided to withdraw from the field.

Despite the severity of Drona's attack, the Pandavas were getting the upper hand. Noticing that his troops were getting demoralized, the guru decided that the moment had come to attack Yudhishthira head on. He sped towards him on his golden carriage at breakneck speed. Standing his ground, Yudhishthira met him with a barrage of barbed arrows, tagged with eagle feathers. But this did not deter Drona. He swept on, as if these were soft feathers raining on him. He attacked with such violence that within minutes Yudhishthira's bow had shot out of his hands.

Full of consternation, Drishtadyumna showered arrows on the guru to prevent Drona from advancing, but to no avail. Even as warriors made a beeline towards them to fend off Drona, he reached so close that a cry resounded across the battlefield, 'Yudhishthira has been captured!'

Just then, Arjuna appeared on the scene. As his chariot dashed across the blood-soaked field strewn with dead bodies, he let loose an unending torrent of arrows from his Gandiva. The arrows sprang from his bow like magic, darkening the air around him. When Drona saw Arjuna approaching, he panicked and retreated post-haste.

Yudhishthira had a lucky escape that day. Thus, when the battle was halted in the evening, despite Drona's brilliant leadership, the Kauravas were despondent. On the other hand, the Pandavas went back to their camp jubilant at their triumph.

Drona had to furnish an apologetic account of his failure to capture Yudhishthira to Duryodhana. 'I almost had him, when Arjuna suddenly appeared. The arrows fell so thick and fast that there was nothing to do but fall back or be killed,' he said ruefully. 'You know that his quiver is inexhaustible. We have to think of a way to draw him away from his brother and keep him engaged in a distant part of the field. If Arjuna can be distracted, I promise to present Yudhishthira as a captive to you tomorrow.'

Susarma, the ruler of Trigartadesh, overheard this conversation. He immediately went and took counsel from his brothers Satyaratha, Satyavarma, Satyaaasu and Satyadharma to search for a way to lure Arjuna from Yudhishthira's side. After much discussion, they decided to take a fearsome pledge called the samsaptaka oath to accomplish this. Then, they went around recruiting soldiers who might be willing to join them. Once they had got a group together, they dressed in garments fashioned out of grass and sat around a fire. They performed all the funeral rites for themselves and swore the following oath: 'We pledge not to turn back from the field of battle till we have slain Arjuna. And if we waver in our resolve and flee from him, let the severest punishment be reserved for us!'

After binding themselves in this suicide pact, the cohort marched southwards, since it was believed that death came from that direction. They bellowed out a challenge to Arjuna, 'O Arjuna! Come and face us if you can!'

Arjuna heard their war cry. He knew he would have to go and do battle with them. 'The samsaptakas are calling me to fight them,' he said to Yudhishthira. 'I have no choice but to accept this challenge. Please allow me to go, dear brother. I will return only after I have finished off each one of them.'

'Arjuna,' Yudhishthira replied with a sigh, 'you well know what Drona is planning. He is a peerless warrior, skilled in all kinds of weaponry. You are the only one who can defeat him. But ... please follow whatever you consider to be the right course of action.'

Arjuna nodded, his face grim. He led Satyajit, a prince of Panchala, forward. 'This intrepid young man is here to guard you. He will take care that you come to no harm.'

Without further ado, Arjuna strode off to mount his chariot and attack the samsaptakas. 'Drive on, dear Krishna,' he said. 'These men know that death awaits them, but they are under the spell of their oath.'

The twelfth day of battle dawned. When Yudhishthira saw his former guru Drona dashing towards him in his golden chariot, he turned to Drishtadyumna who stood beside him. 'See, the brahmin is coming to catch hold of me. Do your best to fend him off.'

When Drona caught sight of the Panchala prince defending Yudhishthira, he veered off in another direction. He knew that his death was foretold at Drishtadyumna's hands, and felt it would be prudent to turn his weapons on others, till another opportunity presented itself. Sooner or later, the tide of battle would bear Drishtadyumna elsewhere. This is exactly what happened. When he saw that the threat had been averted, Drishtadyumna left his brother Satyajit in charge and sped off to another part of the field.

Drona saw that the coast was clear and returned to seize his prey. Young Satyajit fought valiantly, but in the end, unable to match Drona's fury, he fell. However, many other Pandava warriors hurried forward to protect their king. Drona cut them down too. But for all his efforts, by the time the battle was halted for the day, he had been unsuccessful at capturing Yudhishthira.

Despite Susarma's attempts to keep Arjuna engaged, the Kauravas found they had suffered many losses.

Thus, when the trumpets blew to announce the thirteenth day of battle, Yudhishthira sallied on to the field, still a free man. Naturally, Duryodhana's mood was fouler than ever. As Drona stood in the midst of a group of princes discussing the plan for the day, Duryodhana let loose his frustration on the guru. 'Respected teacher,' he snarled, 'you had numerous opportunities to capture Yudhishthira yesterday but you squandered them all. I cannot understand why you behaved in that manner and what reason you have to neglect your promise to me!'

These words cut Drona to the quick. However, he controlled himself and replied in a balanced tone. 'Duryodhana,' he said, 'anyone can see that I am employing all the expertise I possess to seize hold of Yudhishthira. You are making allegations that are below the dignity of a noble ruler like you. I said this earlier and I say it again – Arjuna has to be lured away from Yudhishthira's side. Only then will it be possible to capture the king.'

Once again, the samsaptakas called out to Arjuna and drew him away to fight on the south of the battlefield. The combat that ensued was the most ferocious in the whole war. In the meantime, Drona ranged his forces in the lotus formation and launched a brutal attack on Yudhishthira. This turned out to be an unbeatable challenge for the Pandavas.

The chakravyuh or padmavyuha, as it was also called, was a military formation used to surround and capture an enemy. It was a multi-tiered battle formation that resembled a disc or chakra or a blooming lotus if viewed from above.

It was a formidable formation that began with a semi-circle of two soldiers standing back-to-back, with another such set of soldiers standing at a three-hand distance. In this manner, seven circles were set up. The soldiers in front would advance to take up position on either side of the person they were targeting. They would engage with him briefly and then move forward in front of their target. The next set of soldiers would stand beside the person being attacked and after a brief skirmish, advance ahead and yield place to the third group. Thus, little by little, their victim would be pushed into the middle of the formation, by which time he would find he was surrounded by seven layers of soldiers. When the last level had effectively enclosed their quarry, the soldiers would give a signal to the others and all the soldiers looking outward would turn around to face their target. Only then would the captured enemy realize that he was fatally trapped. The troops could lead their prisoner away while maintaining the circular formation.

Thus, Drona had devised a brilliant strategy to capture Yudhishthira. Worst of all, the art of penetrating this formation and breaking it up was known only to Krishna and Arjuna.

All the greatest fighters among the Pandavas did their best to get into the formation and scatter the tight-knit group, but none of them succeeded. It was a special art and no matter how hard they tried, they could not halt the onward march of Drona's army.

As this formidable mass of soldiers advanced towards him, a desperate Yudhishthira tried to think of a way out of this hopeless situation. A sudden thought flashed into his mind and he immediately sent for Abhimanyu, Arjuna's son from Subhadra, Krishna's sister. Abhimanyu was extremely young, barely sixteen years old, but he had already proved his prowess in battle.

'Dear son,' Yudhishthira said, 'Dronacharya is wreaking havoc amongst our forces. None of us have been able to break through his chakravyuh. If only your father was here! He knows how to penetrate this formation and escape. I have heard that you have some knowledge about this too. Do you think you know enough to end this threat from Drona's forces?'

'Uncle, I know how to break into the chakravyuh,' Abhimanyu said eagerly. 'I have learnt it from my father.' Then he paused. 'The only thing is, I don't know how to get out of it.'

It was said that one day, while Abhimanyu was still in his mother Subhadra's womb, Arjuna was explaining the method of entering this formidable battle formation to her. The unborn child was listening as well. However, after some time Subhadra dozed off, leaving Abhimanyu with incomplete knowledge For this reason, he was unable to hear the complete mantra to escape from the chakravyuh.

'My brave boy!' Yudhishthira's face lit up as he patted Abhimanyu on his shoulder. 'Do not worry about getting out. Just break in and we will follow you and smash them all.'

Bhima nodded enthusiastically. 'I will be close behind you, and the moment you manage to enter, I'll slip in too. Drishtadyumna, Satyaki, the Panchalas, Kekayas and our other allies will follow us. All you need to do is to penetrate the chakravyuh.'

Abhimanyu was a daring and gallant young man. When he heard his uncle Bhima reassure him, he was further motivated to make this attempt and thus earn great praise from his father and uncle, apart from winning laurels in battle.

'Uncle, wait and see, I shall accomplish this feat and prove a worthy son to my father!' he said confidently.

Yudhishthira was deeply moved. 'May you grow in valour and strength, dear boy,' he said, embracing Abhimanyu.

Drona's flag was visible from a distance. 'Drive on, Sumitra,' Abhimanyu said to his charioteer. 'As fast as you can. Carry me to that point.'

'I pray that the gods are watching over you,' the charioteer replied. 'Yudhishthira has set you an extremely dangerous task. You know what a great general Drona is. You are courageous indeed, but he is a wily old fighter.'

'I am Krishna's nephew and Arjuna's son, my friend!' Abhimanyu's face was flushed with the thought of the glory he planned to attain. His eyes gleamed and his arms itched for battle. 'Who else can boast of such a pedigree? Fear itself flees at the sight of me. Our enemies cannot summon up one sixteenth of the strength I possess. Hurry, I am getting impatient to test my skills.'

The charioteer had no choice but to move forward, despite his misgivings.

The sight of Abhimanyu's gilded chariot alarmed the Kauravas. 'It's Abhimanyu!' they cried. 'He has come to break our formation. He is said to be even braver than his father!'

The Pandava forces followed Abhimanyu's chariot close behind. The Kaurava soldiers became apprehensive when they saw the young man dash up to them like a blood-thirsty lion. The tightly wrought formation sagged as Abhimanyu breached it. Drona was filled with consternation as the young man managed to force his way through tier after tier. As the Pandavas entered behind him, the Kauravas began to despair. When Abhimanyu reached the sixth tier, Jayadratha, the king of the Sindhus, moved swiftly to close the gap.

The formation was tightly enclosed again and no one could penetrate it. Brave Abhimanyu was left all alone!

He was, however, wreaking havoc on the Kaurava ranks. His arrows blazed on them, felling soldier after soldier. Duryodhana was infuriated when he saw how Abhimanyu was decimating his army. He dashed forward to face the young man. But Duryodhana was no equal to Arjuna's son. Concerned, Drona entered the fray and rescued his king. Numerous seasoned warriors surrounded Abhimanyu – from Drona to Kripa, Karna to Ashwatthama, Shakuni to Salya. But Abhimanyu sent them back, licking their wounds. The mighty Karna's armour was pierced, Salya was so disabled that he could not move and the others were forced to retreat.

Dronacharya could not control his admiration and exclaimed to Kripa, 'Has there ever been a warrior who can equal this boy in courage?'

Duryodhana heard and lashed out at his general. 'Arjuna was always our guru's favourite,' he snarled. 'No wonder he is not making any attempt to finish off our enemy.'

At this, Dussashana yelled, 'I will finish him off!' He drove his chariot towards Abhimanyu.

The duel was long and furious, as the two skilled charioteers wove their vehicles in circles around each other. In the end, Dussashana was knocked out by Abhimanyu's arrows and his charioteer swiftly bore him away to safety.

The Kauravas were in disarray, just because of one young man. The Paṇdavas were trying to break into the chakravyuh to provide support to their champion. But Jayadratha had closed the breach so effectively that they just could not get through. Yudhishthira smashed his bow with his spear, but Jayadratha took up another. Bhima destroyed the canopy of his chariot but Jayadratha shot his chariot horses down. Thus, the battle continued and the isolated Abhimanyu continued to fight all alone.

Soldier after soldier fell before his onslaught. Seeing their forces in disarray, Duryodhana's son Lakshamana regrouped his men and led a determined attack on Abhimanyu. But this did not daunt Arjuna's valiant son at all. He sent a swift arrow, as lethal as a snake, towards Lakshamana and the young man fell like a tree uprooted in a storm. A cry of grief went up from the Kauravas.

Maddened by the anguish of losing his son, Duryodhana cried, 'Send this evil man to hell!'

Six mighty warriors surrounded Abhimanyu – Drona, Kripa, Ashwatthama, Brihatbala and Kritavarma. They rained arrows upon him but this had no effect.

'His armour is impregnable,' Drona told Karna, 'let us cut away the reins of his horses. While he is floundering, assault him from the back.'

Karna followed his advice. He aimed at Abhimanyu's bow from behind and shattered it. Then he killed his horses and charioteer. But Abhimanyu carried on fighting on foot, lashing out with his sword and shield. Though he was surrounded, he spun like a whirlwind, decimating all who came close to him with his deadly sword. Finally, Drona sent an arrow that broke his sword into two and Karna smashed his shield. Abhimanyu did not skip a heartbeat. He bent and wrenched the wheel from his chariot and used it like a disc.

But how long could Abhimanyu survive, severely outnumbered as he was? One man against dozens of adversaries? His chariot wheel was soon smashed to fragments too. Then Dussashana's son Durmasena leapt on him and struck him down. He battered him with his mace, and the brave Abhimanyu went to his death, fighting till his last breath.

There was great jubilation in the Kaurava ranks. They danced around his corpse, blowing conches, and their cries of victory resounded all over the battlefield.

One of the Kauravas, Yuyutsu, however, was disgusted by this behaviour. 'You have forgotten the code of a righteous warrior,' he lashed out at his companions. 'You surrounded one man and killed him savagely and now you exult instead of hanging your heads in shame. You have invited your own destruction.'

Yuyutsu then flung down his weapons. 'I will not take part in this dishonourable war!' he proclaimed and walked away from the battlefield.

When the Pandavas heard the exultant cries of the Kauravas, a pall of grief descended on them. Yudhishthira lamented loudly, 'What will I say to Arjuna? I was the one who sent his son to an untimely death. How will I console Subhadra? I should have protected Abhimanyu, but I forced him into danger. Has there ever been a bigger fool than me in the universe?'

All the other warriors sat around him, equally overwhelmed with grief, unable to offer any word of consolation.

Then the great sage Vyasa arrived, as he always did when the Pandavas were in despair.

'It is not proper that you, a wise and knowledgeable man, should give way to grief in this manner,' he said. 'Brahma created death so that a balance may be maintained upon earth. It is an inescapable law of existence.'

His words calmed Yudhishthira somewhat.

In the meantime, Arjuna had defeated the samsaptakas and was returning to camp with Krishna. As he approached, a premonition of disaster began to take hold of him. It became stronger as he came closer to the camp.

'There is something wrong, Krishna,' he said. 'There is no music playing and the soldiers look cast down. They are avoiding my gaze. My heart is cold with apprehension. Abhimanyu has not run out to greet me as he always does.'

When they reached Yudhishthira's tent, his worst fears were realized. 'Why are you overcome with gloom?' he asked, casting a questioning glance all around. 'And where is my son? I know that Drona used the chakravyuh today. None of you know the secret of entering it ... Only Abhimanyu did. But I never taught him how to get out of it … is that what happened? Tell me, brothers!'

No one could bear to disclose the terrible truth. Arjuna immediately sensed that a terrible misfortune had befallen him, and broke into loud lamentation. 'All of you were present and you could not save my beloved son from entering Yama's land. What words of consolation can I offer to Subhadra and Draupadi?'

Krishna tried to console him, saying, 'Dearest Arjuna, you well know that a man born as a kshatriya, who lives to wield weapons, constantly courts death. Abhimanyu died young but he has achieved the kind of glory that most warriors can only dream of. What does every soldier long for but an honourable death?' He paused to touch Arjuna gently on his shoulder. 'Remember, the battle has not been won yet. If you give in to your emotions, all your companions will lose heart and Abhimanyu's sacrifice will be in vain.'

Arjuna took a deep breath and sat down heavily. 'Tell me what happened to my son,' he said, in a voice thick with grief.

Yudhishthira narrated the whole episode, not sparing himself for having incited Abhimanyu to breach the chakravyuh. He told Arjuna how Jayadratha had blocked them all and made it impossible to follow Abhimanyu as they had planned, and how the young man had been outnumbered.

This heart-rending account of remorseless butchery was too much for even a seasoned warrior like Arjuna. Yudhishthira had barely finished, when Arjuna toppled from his seat, unconscious.

Immediately, water was sprinkled on his face and attempts made to revive him. After some time, he sat up, his face still bloodless with shock. Then he motioned for some water to be poured into his cupped palm. In a voice, hard as stone, he made a vow: 'I swear to kill this villainous Jayadratha who was the cause of my son's death before sunset tomorrow. If I do not succeed, I will take my own life!'

Saying this, he twanged the string of his Gandiva bow in warning and Krishna blew the Panchajanya conch.

'This is the summons of death to the sons of Dhritirashtra,' Bhima said sombrely and all the others nodded in agreement.

Arjuna's revenge would be deadly indeed. The Kauravas would soon discover what a mistake they had made by targeting Abhimanyu.

The Half-Golden Mongoose

The great war of Kurukshetra came to an end with the defeat of the Kauravas. Yudhishthira was crowned king and he decided to conduct the Ashwamedha yagna or horse sacrifice to commemorate his victory and to expiate all the deeds that went against the spirit of true dharma. Many great princes of the land were invited to attend, and the yagna was celebrated on a magnificent scale.

Apart from the royalty, many brahmins and poor people thronged Yudhishthira's palace, knowing that they would receive generous gifts. Not only was it a grand event but all the rituals were performed strictly in accordance with the rules laid down in the holy books. Numerous people came and left singing praises of the king and remarking that such a great sacrifice had never been performed.

After all the ceremonies were complete, a strange event occurred. A mongoose appeared suddenly and rolled on the ashes of the sacrificial fire in the midst of all the guests and the priests. Then, it let out a loud, mocking laugh in a human voice.

This peculiar happening stunned everyone into silence. The celebratory mood vanished, as a chill descended on the whole gathering.

The mongoose was extremely strange to look at too. One side of its body glistened like gold, but on the other its coat was like any animal of its species. It stared boldly at all the great princes of the land

who were gathered there, under the great silk and brocade tent, and at all the learned brahmins as if it was not in awe of any of them.

The priests exchanged apprehensive glances and began to consult each other, saying, 'Is this an evil spirit that has come to sully our ritual?' 'How are we to explain this phenomenon?'

To their astonishment, the animal began to speak in a human voice. 'Mighty princes and knowledgeable brahmins, please listen carefully to what I'm going to say. You have just completed a great sacrifice. Now you feel that you have accomplished something splendid. King Yudhishthira has fed thousands of hungry souls and no doubt believes he has gained merit to last him for several lives. All of you appear to be extremely proud of this event. Kindly restrain your conceit, because I would like to tell you that this event is insignificant compared to a much greater sacrifice that I personally witnessed.'

Troubled by what they were witnessing, all the mighty kings and princes gazed at this extraordinary animal. Everyone was overwhelmed by the mongoose's boldness and did not dare admonish it for its impertinence.

'Once, a poor brahmin lived in Kurukshetra, who donated merely a measure of barley flour,' the mongoose began. 'This humble gift had far greater significance and gained much more merit than your lavish sacrifice, and the bounty you have scattered along with it.'

This insulting speech struck everyone dumb. That a small animal could be so impudent and speak derisively in a human voice to such an august assembly made everyone uneasy. It felt like a supernatural happening. All of them wanted an explanation for this but hesitated to enter into a conversation with the mongoose. Eventually, one of the brahmins who had been involved in the rituals summoned up the courage to speak to it.

'Who are you and from where have you come, O mongoose? Why do you mock our sacrifice in this manner? It has been performed with strict attention to the rules laid down in the shastras for such rites. The mantras have been chanted correctly and all the oblations offered to the gods as prescribed. Nowhere have we deviated from the norms. All who have attended have received due honour and appropriate gifts. The hungry have been fed, the poor have received generous alms. All the four castes of people are satisfied. Why do you then pour scorn on our sacrifice? Kindly furnish an explanation.'

The mongoose let out another laugh. 'I only speak the truth, O learned brahmin. It is not that I resent the fact that King Yudhishthira has been blessed by the gods. Neither do I envy anyone standing here,' it said boldly. 'This yagna of yours that was celebrated with such pomp and show, is not equal to the charitable act of a poor brahmin. An act that was so great that his wife, son and daughter-in-law were transported to heaven as a reward. This is not a story that I have heard from someone else or concocted. I have witnessed it with my own eyes.'

The mongoose then began to narrate the incident. 'Many years before this great battle of yours was fought, a poor brahmin family lived in Kurukshetra. They fed themselves on grain that they gleaned from the fields. The man, his wife, son, and daughter-in-law, all survived on what they could gather thus. With this small portion of grain, they could only manage one meal a day in the afternoon. Sometimes they were unable to find any grain, so they would fast till the next afternoon. Sometimes they found more than they required, so they gave it away in charity. It was their principle never to keep more for themselves than they needed to fill their bellies.

'Their lives proceeded in this manner for many years when it so happened that a great drought fell upon the land. It did not rain for months and the fields grew parched and no crops could be grown. This famine brought immense hardship on the small family. They toiled day after day and were forced to go hungry most of the time. One day, after roaming the fields for hours under the scorching sun, they were able to collect a measure of barley. They brought it home, ground it into flour, lit a fire and cooked four chapatis from the dough. After saying their prayers and thanking God for this food, they distributed the chapatis and sat down to eat. Just then they heard the cry of a hungry beggar at their door, "Good people, I am about to die, kindly give me some food."

'The father started up and welcomed the beggar. "You have come just in time, good man," he said. "Please accept this chapati. We obtained the flour with our own hard work, so this food is pure and untainted."

'The beggar devoured the chapati but after he had eaten it to the last crumb, he continued to look around with hungry eyes. Noticing this, the wife took the brahmin aside and said, "His hunger has not been sated. It is better that you give him my chapati too."

'"My dear wife," said the brahmin, growing quite agitated. "You are but skin and bone because of the deprivation we have all been suffering. You have starved along with me. Now that we have found a few morsels to keep us alive, how can I allow you to give away this essential sustenance? Even if it gains you much merit, what is the use of suffering so?"

'"You are a learned man," replied his wife, with a smile, "you know that since we have been joined together in marriage all the benefits gained from human activities pertaining to dharma and artha among others, will be credited to both of us. Dear husband, you have been as deprived of food as I am. Please don't think of me as the weaker one. Let me contribute my share of the chapatis so that this man's hunger is appeased and our duty performed."

'The brahmin gave in to his wife's pleading and offered the chapati to the beggar, who ate it up greedily. But it was still not enough to fill his belly. He gazed at them imploringly and said, "Do you have anything more to eat?"

'These words caused great distress to the brahmin. He clutched his forehead in anguish and went to a corner to think. His son, who had overheard all, came to him and said, "Dear father, I will give my chapati to this hungry man. That way our duty towards our guest will be fulfilled."

'The poor brahmin was ready to weep now,' the mongoose continued. "'You are a young man, my boy," he said to his son, brokenly. "Your need for sustenance is greater than mine. Please do not endanger your health. I cannot let you do this."

"'No, father," replied the young man firmly. "It is a son's duty to take care of his aging parents. I should have been the first to offer my chapati. It is also said that the father and son are one, since the son is the reborn version of his father. This chapati is actually yours. Please give it to our guest so that his hunger can be sated and our obligation towards him is complete."

'The father's eyes brimmed over with pride. He laid a hand on his son's head and said, "My heartfelt blessings on you, my dear boy! You have displayed the goodness of heart that I would have hoped from you, as well as exemplary control over your senses."

'He took his son's chapati and offered it to the guest, who devoured it in a minute. Then he asked the brahmin, "Is that all you have? I am still very hungry."

'The brahmin was ready to wail aloud, his anguish was so great. No matter how hard he had tried, he had not been able to satisfy his guest's hunger and thus his dharma would be sullied. His daughter-in-law, who happened to be pregnant, had been watching all along.

'Gaunt and frail as she was, she approached her father-in-law and said, "Dear father, please take my chapati and let me contribute my share to feeding our hungry guest. Please, allow me this opportunity to perform a good deed."

'The brahmin was utterly cast down when he heard this. "My child, just look at you – you are pale and weak from hunger yourself and yet you want to share the one chapati you have with this man. Think of the child you are carrying in your womb. It needs sustenance too. Do not even dream of giving away your food!"

'But the daughter-in-law persisted. "You are my guru, my teacher," she said. "I beg of you to recall that even an unborn child, be it girl or boy, possesses certain obligations and I, as its mother, have the right to decide what is beneficial for it. Our dharma is my child's dharma. Therefore, you must allow me to contribute this chapati on both our behalf so that our guest may not go hungry from our door."

'"May heaven shower all its blessings on you, best of daughters-in-law!" the brahmin exclaimed, overcome by her sacrifice. He offered the chapati to the beggar, saying, "Dear sir, this is all we have left. We hope this will satisfy you."

'The guest ate the chapati with great relish. Then he said, "My good man, blessed is your hospitality. My hunger is fully appeased now. You have given without thinking of yourself, whatever you possessed. You did not let the extremity of your hunger dim your thoughts, or your attachment to your family. And they all stood by you and put my need before their own. There can be no greater sacrifice than yours. Mighty kings conduct extravagant sacrifices, but nothing can equal what you have done by giving away these four dry chapatis to feed a starving man, even though you yourselves were in dire need of food. See, observing your sacrifice, the gods themselves are showering flowers from heaven upon you."

'Sure enough, as the kind-hearted family looked up, confounded, the chariots of the gods rolled down from the heavens and bore the generous four straight to the heavens.

'I had been drawn by the aroma of food being cooked,' continued the half-golden mongoose. 'And I witnessed the whole episode. How I marvelled at the sight of these hospitable people being blessed by the gods! Then I smelt a wonderful fragrance. It rose from the ashes of the fire in which the chapatis had been cooked. I was overcome by an impulse to roll in those blessed ashes and when I did, to my astonishment, that half of my body turned golden. However, when I rolled over on the other side, I found that all the ashes had been used up so my fur retained its natural colour.

'Since then, whenever I hear about a sacrifice being conducted and food being given away in charity, I hurry there to roll in the ashes. The sad fact is that to this date, I have not come across any ashes so blessed that they can turn the other half of my coat to gold. Thus, I remain a half-golden mongoose.'

The mongoose disappeared as mysteriously as it had arrived, leaving King Yudhishthira and all the high-born kings, princes and nobles, and all the learned priests sunk in thought. The mongoose had made them aware of the true spirit of sacrifice, which was not to gain praise and impress others, but to give up even your life's sustenance to benefit someone who was in greater need.

Glossary

Adharma: That which is against the code of dharma or righteous behaviour

Akshay Patra: Vessel of plenty; the magical pot that provided an inexhaustible supply of food to the Pandavas during their exile in the forest

Apsara: Celestial singer and dancer at the court of Indra, king of the gods.

Angiras: Venerated sage, father of Brihaspati, guru of the gods

Artha: Financial security; one of the four goals of existence in Hindu philosophy

Ashram: Hermitage, monastery

Asura: Demi gods engaged in warfare with the gods; demons

Ashwamedha: Horse sacrifice, conducted to prove a king's supremacy over other rulers.

Astra: Weapon

Bhagavad Gita: 700-verse Sanskrit scripture, a dialogue between Krishna and Arjuna at the beginning of the Mahabharata war in which Krishna exhorts a hesitant Arjuna to fulfill his duty as a kshatriya through selfless action

Bhairava: The fierce manifestation of Shiva, associated with destruction

Brahmacharya: The stage of life connected with education, when self-control and celibacy was practised

Brahmin: One belonging to the highest caste of priests and teachers in Hinduism

Chakravyuh: Military formation resembling a labyrinth

Deva: God

Dharma: The right way of living; righteous conduct

Gandharvas: Heavenly beings proficient in music

Gandiva: Arjuna's celestial bow, made by Brahma and presented to Arjuna by Agni

Guru: Teacher

Guru Dakshina: Gift given to a guru for imparting education

Kamadhenu: The miraculous wish-fulfilling cow who provides her owner with whatever she/he might desire; also known as the mother of all cows

Kauravas: Descendants of King Kuru, more commonly known as the hundred sons of King Dhritirashtra of Hastinapur and Queen Gandhari

Kshatriya: The second or warrior caste in Hinduism

Mritasanjivani mantra: A powerful mantra that restored the dead to life again

Naga: Semi-divine being, part human, part snake

Naraka: Hell

Pandavas: The five sons of King Pandu of Hastinapur

Rajasuya: Vedic ritual performed by kings to prove their supremacy

Rakshasa: Enormous beings with powers of illusion, mostly violent and bloodthirsty but sometimes good

Reincarnation: The rebirth of a soul in another body

Rishi: Learned sage

Sanyasa: Renunciation of worldly life and desire; the last stage of human existence

Shloka: Indian verse form; couplet

Swarga: Heavenly world where righteous souls are believed to live before their next incarnation

Swayamvara: Ancient Indian practice in which a girl chose her husband from a group of suitors

Upanishads: Ancient Indian texts that were part of the Vedas, containing the main philosophic concepts of Hinduism, also called Vedanta or the last chapters of the Vedas

Vedas: Oldest Hindu sacred texts in Sanskrit; there are four Vedas – the Rigveda, Yajurveda, Samaveda and Atharvaveda

Yadavas: The descendants of the mythical King Yadu, Krishna belonged to this clan

Yagna: A Hindu ritual performed in front of a fire with the chanting of mantras

Yakshas: Nature spirits, sometimes benign at other times mischievous

Yoga: a set of physical, mental and spiritual practices that originated in ancient India to promote good health, well-being and spiritual discipline

Yuga: In Hinduism, an era with a cycle of four ages – starting with Satyuga to Tretayuga, Dwaparyuga and Kaliyuga. Each age sees a decline in virtue in human beings.

More from the House of Harper series

A BASKETFUL OF ANIMAL TALES:
Stories from the Panchatantra

Sreelata Menon
Illustrated by Megha Punater

'Give me six months, and I will teach your sons how to live wisely. They will make you proud,' said the Pandit. And thus was born the great book of animal stories – The Panchatantra.

Cunning jackals, stupid crocodiles, lumbering elephants and clever mice. Foolish fish and clever crows, quick-witted monkeys and dim-witted lions. Pit your wits against them in this feast of animal stories! Though ancient, the stories from the Panchatantra remain as modern as any new story today and have been retold again and again through the ages.